Relatively Familiar

Accidental Familiar 2

By Belinda White

Prologue: Arc's Story . . . The Beginning

When I first sensed the large and unmoving lump behind me in my bed, I totally freaked. In a logical and manly way, of course.

After leaping from the bed and wrapping my robe around my naked body, I whirled around to glare at the lump. From this angle, I could see it was a human-shaped lump with a crown of silky golden hair.

Sonya.

At least the who part was solved. Now for the how.

My home is very well warded. In fact, warding homes is one of my magic specialties. It wouldn't be bragging to say that I was one of the very best at it. Well, it might be a bit of bragging, but that didn't make it any less true. I was the master. No one I knew could even come close to the impenetrable wards I could create.

Only now, apparently, someone had penetrated them. The ones on my own home, no less. The strongest I had ever done. Or so I had thought, anyway.

The question remained, how did she manage to bypass my magical security system and gain entrance to not only my home but my bedroom as well? Not that she hadn't tried that feat before, because she had. Many times. It had been Sonya's main goal in life to tarnish my perfect ward record.

Not for any bad purpose. Rather, just to prove that she could.

As witches go, the two of us were pretty much equal when it came to sheer power. It's just that our powers are very different. Mine focused on protection abilities. Sonya's powers were on the destructive side. The difference between Earth and Fire.

It made for a rocky, yet highly invigorating, relationship.

Now that she had managed to break through my protections, I would never be able to forget it. She would make sure of that.

I sat in the chair by the bed, waiting for her to turn and flash me that brilliant winning smile. But she didn't. After a few minutes of waiting, the worry started to creep in.

No way could Sonya hold the gloating in this long. Something was wrong.

Walking around to the other side of the bed, I freaked for the second time. This time probably not nearly so manly, as I'm pretty sure I screamed a little.

Sonya wouldn't be gloating about breaking my wards. Not now, not ever.

Sonya was dead.

I'm a damn powerful witch. The name Archimedes Mineheart Junior meant something in the circle of witches. But even I couldn't make a dead body disappear. Or move it across time or space either.

Which was a very bad thing, because it was just at that moment of discovery that all my homes' wards went off at once.

I was surrounded.

From the flashing red-and-blue lights coming through my bedroom curtains, I was guessing the police. And as the local police knew exactly who and what I was, chances were very good that there would be a couple witches' council members too.

My wards would stand up to a single witch any day of the week, but multiple ultra-powered masters of the craft? My home would be breached within a matter of minutes.

I couldn't spirit the body away, and I couldn't just disappear myself either.

Or could I?

As luck would have it, and because of circumstances completely beyond my control, my familiar was not with me at the moment. But they wouldn't know that, would they?

As the last of my protection spells fell, I took one final look at Sonya's body, trying to commit everything about the sight to memory. Then I opened the bedroom window and cast the transformation spell.

They didn't even bother to knock. One minute I had a front door, and the next minute I didn't. An entire squad of heavily armored police officers entered the room. Once they declared the place clear, the witches entered.

Part of me really, really wanted to make my exit at that moment, but the other part was hoping for some small clue as to just what the hell was going on. The curious part of me won out. Unfortunately, there is that old saying about what curiosity does to cats.

Seeing the three council members enter gave me a moment's pride. Most times, they only sent two. My reputation must be even stronger than I had thought.

3

There wasn't much that could withstand a trinity of witches. Not ones with their power. A single witch, no matter how powerful, would never stand a chance.

There were two ways I could play this. I could try to sneak out the front door and past them. But that might draw more suspicion than I wanted. They might decide to try to stop me, and the chase would be on. There would probably end up being a chase, anyway, but I wanted as much of a head start as I could get.

Taking a deep breath, I arched my now white and furry back and hissed for all I was worth. A couple officers jumped at my ferocious battle cry, but the witches just smirked.

"That's just his familiar," Tabitha said. She was the actual second-in-command of the entire council. They must really think I was a threat if they sent her.

Just what the bloody hell was going on here? I waited until the last of the police officers had entered the bedroom, which they did quickly after finding the entryway empty. The witches stood back to back in the center of the front room and closed their eyes.

Crap. They were casting feelers out for my magical signature. Wouldn't they be surprised to find it right there in front of them?

I ran as fast as my little furry legs would carry me, but not toward the door. I darted back into the bedroom and up and onto the half-open windowsill. Thank the Goddess I had thought to open it. Hovering for a second on the narrow sill, I eyed the tree just outside the window. I'd seen Baxter make the leap dozens of times, but then, he was a cat through and through. I was a man in a cat suit.

The mental debate was still on when the first cry from the witches came from the living room. "Stop that cat!"

It was now or never.

I jumped.

Chapter 1

There were times when keeping a promise was hard. This wasn't one of them.

My promise to Arc, my new accidental familiar, was an easy one for me to make good on. Mostly because it gave me a reason to leave home for a while. Home was confusing right now.

Aunt Opal was being uncharacteristically hovering, and my best friend Opie had taken a bit of a runner on me after seeing me do a massive magical attack. I couldn't really blame either of them, I guess. Both witnessed my new and previously unknown ability. It was scary as heck.

It scared me too.

Helping Arc clear his name back in Indiana would give me a chance to make some things up to him, plus give me the distance I needed from my family and Opie to think things through. Find my new status quo.

Arc had even promised to help me with that. He was proving to be a good friend too. I really needed one right now.

I glanced over at the gorgeous dark-haired man in the passenger seat beside me. "So, you want to go over what happened one more time for me? From the top this time?"

He'd already given me the short version. Someone had killed his ex-lover Sonya and was trying, successfully it seemed, to pin the murder on him. Right now, that was all I knew. I needed the whole story, and preferably before we got there.

Or before the witches' council showed up and arrested us both. Him for a murder he didn't commit, and me for harboring and helping a known fugitive.

Truthfully, I was a little surprised they hadn't shown up already. They were well known for their ability to track down magical renegades. It sounded weird, but in a way that had me worried too. Were they waiting for something before making their move? Were they secretly tracking us?

At first, I thought he wasn't going to answer me. The silence lengthened. I let it. Losers speak first. It was something my cousin Ruby had taught me a long time ago.

"I really don't know much," he said, finally. "I woke up one morning to find I wasn't alone in my bed. Which was totally strange, because I had been when I went to sleep, and the wards on my apartment were still fully in place as far as I could tell."

I'd seen his wards in action. They were pretty dang impressive.

"Sonya?"

He nodded and then looked back out the window, not meeting my eyes. Normally, I'd take that as a sign of evasion or untruthfulness, but I could tell he was hurting. Arc had truly cared for Sonya. They might not have been a real couple, but according to him, they'd been friends pretty much all their lives.

Kind of like Opie and me. And there was the pain again. I brushed it to one side. I'd deal with it later.

"Was she alive?"

"No. I thought so at first." He gave a dry laugh. "She was always trying to break my wards. I thought she'd finally succeeded and that any minute, the gloating would start." Closing his eyes, he leaned heavily against the back of his seat. "At the time, I thought that was the worst thing that could have happened. Man, was I wrong."

That was bad. Not only had someone broken through the Mineheart Fireworks Ward, they had also managed to place a dead body right in the bed next to him without him waking up. That would be kind of hard for anyone to believe.

Even me, if Arc hadn't been under a truth spell when he'd told us he was innocent. And Ruby's spells rarely missed their mark.

"Could you tell how she died?"

He shook his head. "No. Not really. But her head didn't look quite . . . right." A shiver passed over him, and he swallowed hard. "I'll never forget the look on her face. She'd seen it coming, and it had terrified her."

A couple minutes passed in silence. The drive from Wind's Crossing to Oak Hill, Indiana wasn't an overly long one. If we followed the speed limits, which I sure as heck would be as I had a fugitive in my car, it would take no more than an hour. We still had time, and I didn't feel the need to rush him.

Arc took a deep, catching breath. "Of course, that's when the council showed up." He threw a glance over at me. "I guess I probably should have told you they sent a trinity. Your Aunt Opal was one of them."

The car swerved slightly as I looked over at him. He had failed to mention that part before. That was so not good. And here he'd been staying in our house within mere yards of the woman for days now. That had to have taken guts.

The council worry notched up a little. I didn't know many council members, but I knew my aunt. She was good. Very good. How had she not known the man she was looking for was right upstairs in her own house?

It didn't make any sense.

"Sorry I didn't tell you before. I thought maybe it would complicate things."

Well, yeah. But what was there to do about that now? "How did you get away from a witches' trinity that had Opal as a member?" That feat was an impressive one. Trinities were powerful in themselves. Ones with Opal in them I had thought were pretty much unstoppable.

"Can't you guess?"

Oh, yes. The cat thing. When I'd first met Arc, he'd been in an animal shelter one town over from Oak Hill. He'd been tiny and furry at the time. That's what had led to the whole accidental familiar thing. Just as much his fault as it was mine, if you asked me.

"Even as a cat, it's pretty darn impressive that you got past them."

"If it hadn't been for the big oak tree outside my bedroom window, I wouldn't have." He smiled. "I'd seen Baxter, my familiar, come in and out of that window via that tree many times." Then he got pensive. "I wonder how Baxter is doing right now. How could I have forgotten him for this long?"

"Well, it's not like you've been on vacation or something." I paused. "Was he in the apartment when you left?"

"No. He was out wandering. He does that at night." He was quiet for a minute. "He's walked with me over to my uncle's before. You think maybe he could have found his way over there?"

He was asking me? "I really wouldn't know." I smiled at him. "You're the first cat I ever really spent any time with, and you know how that turned out."

"That's right. You sneezed at the shelter. And you were wearing one of those face masks too. Are you really that allergic to cats?"

I nodded. Not something I was proud of, but also not something I could deny. Well, I could deny it . . . until a cat showed up. Then my sneezing and watery eyes would give me away pretty dang quickly.

"I feel for you. That must have been rough growing up." He was back to looking out the window. "Me and Baxter are pretty tight. Until I went off and abandoned him."

"If he's your familiar, then he'll have some idea of what's been going on, right? And if your uncle lives that close, I'm sure if Baxter didn't find him, he'd find Baxter." I hesitated. "Your uncle would do that, wouldn't he?" I mean, I know Aunt Opal would go looking for Yorkie Doodle if anything ever happened to Ruby. Goddess forbid.

That earned me a brilliant smile. "Yeah, he would. Thanks. I feel better now."

"Good, so get back to the story. All that work you did back home on my computer. Did you find anything useful?"

Arc made a face. "Just that they're pretty sure I'm guilty of killing Sonya." He rubbed a hand down his face and went back to leaning heavily on his seat with his eyes closed. "Can't say I blame them, really. I mean, the Mineheart wards aren't known for being breachable. No way is anyone going to believe I slept through them going off."

"I'm pretty sure they didn't go off." He just looked at me. "Well, for one thing, they were still up when you found Sonya, right?"

He nodded, his expression thoughtful.

"And for another, if they had gone off, I'm fairly certain the neighbors would have heard it."

"So, we're back to the question of how did they get through the wards without setting them off."

"Looks that way." I glanced down at the fuel gauge. I hadn't thought to fill up before we left, and we were running kind of low. Good thing, too, because I had the opposite problem. I'd been drinking far too much. I pulled over to the side of the road and looked at him. "You need to change into your alternate persona so I can get gas and take a restroom break."

"Hey! I've gotta go too."

That was a dilemma. But for him, not me.

"Sorry, but we're far too close for you to show yourself in public." I pointed off into the woods. "Why don't you change into your cuter, furrier self and go out in the woods?"

He just looked at me with his eyebrows drawn together. "And how am I supposed to wipe with paws?"

"Seriously? You can't wait to do that until we get to the hotel?"

"I've kind of needed to go for a while now. I just didn't want to say anything because I figured I'd get the 'you should have gone before we left home' lecture. Only I didn't need to then. Now I do."

Since I'd already admitted to having a need for the bathroom myself, I couldn't really complain. But that didn't mean I wasn't going to stick to my guns here. There was far too much at stake.

"You need to suck it up, change, and go out into the woods by the road to do your business." I held up a hand to stop him from butting in. "When you're done, find a nice clear patch of grass and scoot your bottom on it. I've seen cats do that in videos." Found it pretty dang hilarious, too, but I didn't think saying that would help my case.

He glared at me, but then he opened his car door, changed, and ran off into the woods.

I was really hoping he wouldn't take a long time just out of spite. It would be like him, and my needs were getting a bit desperate. Before long, I'd have to go into the trees myself. But there was a town just up ahead, and I was holding out for a nice, flushable toilet.

Unfortunately, while I was waiting for Arc to finish his business, the council showed up.

Chapter 2

At least it wasn't a trinity this time. It was just a single witch. One I didn't recognize. I only knew she was council because they always insisted on wearing that stupid hat. No non-council witch would be caught dead in the thing, but for them, it was a status symbol. Well, all of them but Opal. At least my aunt had better taste than that.

She wheeled her car in front of mine sideways, like she was somehow blocking me from getting away. Yeah, lady, I thought, there is such a thing as reverse, you know. But then, I didn't know how many others were on their way to join the party.

Jumping out of her car, she pointed her wand at me. "Don't move."

I just looked at her. Yes, I was worried, but I sure as heck wasn't going to let her see that. There was a small chance that as long as Arc stayed in the woods, we'd be fine.

Of course, she had to have some reason for pointing that blasted wand at me, so maybe the chance was a bit slimmer than I'd originally thought.

"Is it against the law now to stop alongside the road for a breather?" I was going to play it cool for just as long as I could. Maybe I could buy Arc enough time to get the bloody heck out of Dodge. Without him there, she really didn't have a thing to pin on me. Right?

She looked me up and down and then glanced in the car. Her eyes lit up when she saw the carrier in the back seat. "Where is your cat?"

Dang. I should have stowed the stupid thing in the trunk. "He needed to go to the bathroom."

She gave me a smug smile. "And you trusted him enough to just let him go alone?"

I met her eyes straight on and shrugged. "Would your familiar run away from you?"

If I hadn't been staring straight into her eyes, I would have missed it. But there for just a shadow of a second, an emotion had flickered across them. She recovered quickly; I'd give her that.

"Can I ask why you seem to think I'm a danger? I'd really appreciate it if you could point that thing somewhere else."

All that got me was a sneer. "Yes, you would like that, wouldn't you? And I think you know what I'm here for. Or should I say who I'm here for? Your magical signature just set off the road wards we have set up."

I was really hoping that Arc was getting some distance between himself and us. A second later, I knew that wasn't the case. He came out of the trees and walked right up to us.

Just how stupid was he?

She glanced down at him and then back up at me. "You say this cat is your familiar?" The seed of doubt was there. "Prove it."

Arc had told me that he was very limited as to what he could do in cat form, but luckily, he had this covered. A thin blue line of magic formed between us.

"Is this proof enough? Or did you want to ask my aunt about my new familiar? I think you might know her. Opal Ravenswind?"

I hated bringing Opal into this, but I was desperate. And I was actually kind of confused as to why she hadn't already just nabbed us both and arrested us in the council's name. It was dangerous, but I was starting to have a glimmer of hope.

The witch looked at me for a moment. "You're Amethyst Ravenswind?"

"I am." I pointed down to Arc at my feet. "And that is my new familiar. Now would you kindly tell me why you say my magical signature set off your road wards? Am I wanted for some crime?"

She was trying to hide it, but I could tell she was more than a little confused. "You did set off our wards, but it wasn't a one hundred percent match for who we were looking for. It was close enough, though, that I had to check it out." She paused as if she was considering how much to tell me. "I don't suppose you are any kind of relation to Archimedes Mineheart?"

"Isn't he one of the lawyers at Mineheart Law? If so, then I was actually going to see him tomorrow."

The smug look was back. "And what would a niece of Opal Ravenswind be doing going to see an Earth witch lawyer?"

I tilted my head and looked at her. "Since when does the council have the right to ask anything about my personal business? If you have a subpoena, I'd love to see it right about now. Otherwise, I'm taking my cat and leaving. We're done here."

It was a harrowing few minutes, but she didn't try to stop me as I put Arc in the carrier and backed my car up. I kept expecting a magical bolt of lightning to come flying out of the end of her wand and flatten all my tires, but it didn't happen.

We got away clean but very confused. She had us and just let us go? If we set off those wards, and I was fairly certain we did, then it was Arc who had done that, not me. And why wouldn't his signature be a one hundred percent match?

What the heck was going on here? Or was she only toying with us?

***

After a quick stop off at the next gas station for a fill-up and an empty out, we raced to the hotel. I had left that decision up to Arc, as he knew the area and I didn't. He had chosen a little rundown place just outside of town.

His reasoning was that no self-respecting Mineheart would be caught dead there, so it wouldn't be on the council's radar. I wasn't sure about that, but it met my simple requirements, so I was okay with it. The Oak Hill Lodge accepted pets, and it was dirt cheap. The money thing was important, as my last job had only paid me with this car, which quickly became an expense, what with insurance and gas and everything else.

When I'd first gotten it, it had been covered in nasty and vulgar slogans and pictures from the previous owner's construction business. Most of them were now covered by custom decals I'd ordered. Yet another drain on my meager finances, but so worth it. Now I didn't have old ladies cursing at me if I parked the Challenger in their sight. That got old quick.

The Lodge was everything I expected it to be. I drove into the small gravel parking lot and gazed upon our temporary new home—a long stretch of blue-painted wood that held six doors and precisely six windows. The paint was peeling, and a couple of the doors didn't look like they would actually be successful in keeping anything out that wanted in. Like a mouse. No way were they putting me in one of those units. I upped my requirements for staying there by one: a sturdy door. Wards would only do so much.

I went to the office and paid for a full week up front. It ticked me off when they charged me a pet deposit, but what could I do? I paid it, got the key, grabbed Arc's carrier, and unlocked the door into our room.

For a minute, I just stood there, kind of in shock. I took a step back and glanced down the row of wood, doors, and windows in disrepair and then back into the room. The difference was astounding. I could get used to this place. Obviously, the owner's time and money went on the inside rather than the outside.

It was clean and homey with two single beds, a loveseat with an ottoman, a larger flat-screen television, and an antique dresser that would have Aunt Opal salivating. For that matter, she'd be drooling over the nightstands by the beds too. Not to mention the old oaken table and chairs in the corner.

The room was absolutely adorable. So much so that I took out my phone and snapped a quick picture. I'd get one of the outside, too, just for the heck of it. But I could do that later. Now we had to get down to business.

After bringing in the bags from the car—it was tiring being the only human in the group allowed outside—and securely locking the door, I looked to Arc and gave him the nod. When the blue haze lifted, the gorgeous naked man was there again. It would be nice if he could figure out how to at least keep his shorts on when he was in cat mode, but according to him, it wouldn't work. With the little, and disastrous, experience I'd personally had with working magic, I had to take his word for it.

He turned his back to me and dressed quickly. Then he flopped onto one of the beds and covered his eyes with one of his hands.

"This is so very bad."

"I take it you know that witch? Was she one of the trinity that showed up at your place that day?"

Arc nodded. "Yes. And it's even worse than that. Her name is Patricia Bluespring, and she happens to be my father's first ex-wife. She has always had it out for my family. Nothing would make her happier than to put me in some magic-draining hole. Well, other than putting my father in there with me."

"Crapsnackles." I was quiet for a minute as I thought about it. "If she hates your family that badly, it wouldn't hurt to put her on our list of suspects."

He lifted his arm and opened one eye to look at me. "Why would she kill Sonya?" Then he bolted upright on the bed. "Dash it all, I think you might be right. Sonya told me she had dirt on someone in the council, but she wouldn't tell me who. If it was Patricia and she got too close, then that could have gotten her killed."

"And who better to pin it all on than a Mineheart, right?"

Arc's eyes were flashing from side to side as if trying to keep up with his racing thoughts. "Even if it wasn't her, that's the first motive I've come up with for anybody to hurt Sonya. She was free-living, but she never went out of her way to hurt anyone. Quite the opposite. I've been racking my brain, trying to come up with a reason, and here you've given me one the first day into the case."

His eyes finally stopped on mine. He was giving me a fierce grin. "I think you're going to make one heck of a detective."

"Yeah, well, I have to finish the schooling and other requirements before I can hang out my shingle." I paused. I really hated to burst his bubble this soon. "And as much as I hate to say this, the killer is rarely the first one you think of. We need to start brainstorming."

He gave me a nod, but I could tell he'd just be going through the motions. In his mind, he already knew who the killer was. Patricia Bluespring.

I still had my doubts. For a council witch, she didn't strike me as all that powerful.

And it would have taken a powerful witch indeed to make it through the Mineheart Fireworks Ward without all hell breaking loose.

We had to keep looking. But the council membership might not be a bad place to start.

Chapter 3

I had two visits to make the first full day in town. Because of the circumstances, they were both to be single goes, no Arc. Most places just weren't all that friendly when you brought your cat along for the ride.

My first choice of stops was Firestorm United. That was Sonya Ignacio's last place of employment. People who work together know things about each other. I was hoping I could make friends with one of them and get them talking. It was a plan, anyway.

But the Minehearts deserved to be first on the list, so they got bumped up to the top. I'd told Patricia Bluespring that I was visiting Archimedes Mineheart Senior on a personal matter. That was more than true. We knew the council wasn't exactly forthcoming in their techniques. I would think it safe to bet that they had the law office under some kind of magical surveillance. So we had devised a plan.

I wasn't going in as a friend of Arc's. I was visiting as a client. I'd even scheduled an appointment. We really didn't want to leave anything to chance.

When I left the hotel, I was dressed in business casual clothing. No jeans, which was super out of the norm for me. In their place was a nice second-hand pair of dress pants topped with a dressy sweater. It was my standard interviewing outfit. And yes, it had gotten a lot of use in the last couple of years.

Taking a deep breath, I parked the car in the lot behind the law office. I would have rather parked on the street, but the decals didn't cover quite all the slogans, and I tried to hide it as much as possible. Parking in the farthest spot from the door would have to do.

I could do this. I just had to keep telling myself that. I'd taken an acting class in high school. Come to find out, I wasn't very good at it. This was different, though. I only had an audience of one. And however many council members happened to be watching at the time. That was the nerve-racking part. Almost like being on television.

The receptionist greeted me and took me back to a very stylish corner office. As the senior partner, Archimedes Mineheart had the office's prime real estate. There was even a small patio, with a fountain and everything, outside his window. Quite striking and classy. And no doubt very expensive. It was a good thing I wasn't a client for real. These were lawyers I could never afford on my budget.

An older Arc stood as I walked in behind the receptionist. For an older man, he was every bit as gorgeous as his son. If that was how Arc was going to age, Ruby should snatch him up quick.

"Ms. Ravenswind?" He reached his hand over the desk, and we shook as the woman returned to her post as sentry guard. I noticed that she closed the door behind her. Good.

"Please, call me Amie, Mr. Mineheart." I gave him a smile and reached into my bag for the sheath of papers we had prepared. Most of them were printouts of random stuff we got off the internet to fill pages. The top sheet was all that mattered.

"Amie . . . short for Amethyst, is it not?" His smile was quite breathtaking. No wonder his office was so popular. Women would divorce their husbands just to get to work with this man.

"That's right. You probably know my family is pretty well known for being witches. It's a family tradition to name all the children after gemstones. Personally, I think I got lucky."

He laughed, and a shiver ran over my skin. A good shiver. A laugh like that could do things to a woman. "I think so too." He started to say something, then hesitated. When he spoke again, I didn't think it had anything to do with what he had been going to say. "So, Amie, what can our little firm help you with today?"

I glanced down at my stack of papers and tried to remember my acting lessons. "Well, you see, my grandmother passed on a few years ago, and in her will, she left a very . . . powerful . . . heirloom to my cousin. Now she did that because at the time, it was thought I didn't have any magic, but that has since been proven wrong. I want to know if there is any way I can contest the will."

Placing the papers on his desk, I pushed them toward him. He didn't even look at them. Senior looked very disappointed. His eyes lowered, and he took a deep breath. "I see." His fingers drummed on his desk for a minute before he looked back up at me. "I'm sorry, Ms. Ravenswind,"—no more Amie for me—"but I'm afraid I can't help you. It would be next to impossible to contest a will that old."

Okay, there was a problem. Our plan wouldn't work if he wouldn't look at the dang papers.

"Actually, I think I've found a pretty good loophole." I tapped the first page. "If you'll just take a look at this, I think you'll see what I mean."

He sighed, but my words did the trick. His eyes traveled down to where my finger rested on the page. Right on Arc's signature.

I might not be any good at acting, and I'm not at all sure my performance was cutting any muster with the invisible council, but Mr. Archimedes Mineheart Sr. was a master. He could have been a star. His looks would have cinched it.

Other than a flash of recognition when he saw his son's name, there was nothing to show any kind of emotional involvement in the papers before him. He took a minute to read the short note, then even went so far as to flip through the pages behind it. Obviously, he knew as well as we did that his every move was being watched. Or at least suspected it was.

Finally, he swallowed and looked up at me. His mask for the camera was still in place, but I could see just the smallest hint of relief in his eyes. "I see what you mean. Yes, this could indeed be a very interesting case. I truly appreciate you bringing it to us first."

"From what I've heard, you all are the best. This ring means a lot to me, and I think I deserve it every bit as much as Ruby does."

"Well, I'll certainly see what I can do. In the meantime . . .." He pulled a business card out of the holder on his desk and scrawled something on the back. "Here is the name and phone number of the man in our firm who I think would be perfect for this one. He's out of the office today, but give him a call as soon as possible. I know he'll have a lot of questions for you."

I tucked the card into my pocket and stood. "I'll be sure to do that." I didn't want to risk reading it there. As I've said, my acting skills are nowhere near his level of excellence. I'd hate to blow it now.

He reached across the desk, and this time his handshake felt a whole lot more personal. But when his eyes started getting moist, I knew I had to get out of there. Fast.

All that emotion was going to have to be released soon. Hopefully, he'd make it until he was off the stage.

If that was even possible for him.

***

Needless to say, the hasty scrawling on the back of that business card wasn't the name and phone number of another attorney. It was an address.

Torn between going to the offices of Firestorm United Demolition and following through on this, I decided to do a quick drive-by to check it out first. What I found kind of surprised me.

The house the address led me to wasn't in a ritzy, upscale, happening neighborhood. For the Minehearts, that was what I would have expected. Not to say that the house was rundown or in a bad neighborhood, because it wasn't. In fact, if I had the money to purchase a home of my own, should that ever become a priority for me, this was the sort of home I'd want.

The outside was a dusty red brick with stone surrounding the windows and door. The roof was topped with old-fashioned wooden shingles, and the front porch stretched from one corner of the house to the next. One end of the porch held a comfy porch swing, and the other end was home to an old metal glider. Plus, whoever owned this house was a definite lover of nature. Flower and herb beds abounded, and as I recognized a lot of the variety of plants, I knew the inhabitant had to be a witch.

In short, it was the perfect home for a functioning, if somewhat reclusive, witch. I say reclusive because the house was sitting on a rather large lot and surrounded by towering pine trees. I was very curious as to what the backyard looked like. Maybe someday soon, I'd find out.

While I was sitting outside the house, alternating my stares between the house and the card and trying to figure out what to do, an older woman stepped out onto the porch. My heart instantly went out to her. She reminded me so much of my grandmother. The woman was short, not an inch over five feet, if that, and was a bit on the heavy side. Believe me when I say she made it work. I think a part of me fell in love with her before we'd even spoken.

Not that the words took all that long to come.

"Are you coming in or what?"

I swallowed and climbed out of the car. It made total sense that Mr. Mineheart would have warned her somehow that I might be coming. Might as well find out why while I was here.

"I can't stay long. I'm expected somewhere else soon." A little white lie, but it set the groundwork to get out fast if I needed to use it.

She just nodded. "Figured you'd be pretty busy right now." The woman stepped back into the house and left the door open for me to follow her.

I did. Normally, I'd feel awkward going into the house of someone I'd never met before. Especially in the type of situation I currently found myself in. This kind of felt like . . . coming home. Which was weird, to say the least.

"Lemonade, tea, or soda?"

My eyes went from the crocheted doilies—so much like my grandma's—back to her. "Lemonade would be great, thank you."

She came back out and handed me one of the two tall glasses she carried, then motioned for me to take a seat. Again, I complied, taking an experimental sip as I did. Some people made their lemonade far too sour. Not her. This was absolutely perfect.

"My name is Lily Hilton, but please just call me Lily." She winked at me. "I'm a special friend of the Minehearts'. All of them, in fact, but especially Merlin." Her voice softened as she said the name.

"Merlin?"

"Yes, dear. You probably haven't met him yet. He's an attorney at the firm too. Archimedes' older brother and Arc's uncle." Her brows drew together. "We've all been so very worried about him. First the council finding Sonya, and then him dropping off the face of the earth like that. Can I ask how he's doing?"

I hesitated and glanced around. If the council had bugged the law office, what was stopping them from watching this place too?

She saw my glance and smiled. "Don't worry about the council here, sweetie. This place is warded and guarded against intrusion of any kind. Seven ways to Sunday, in fact." Lily looked around her little room, and a small amount of pride crept into her voice. "This little house is probably the safest house in the world thanks to the Minehearts." Another wink. "And maybe just a little help from me."

"I thought from your gardens that you had to be a witch."

"Oh yes, indeed I am. But not an elemental like your family or my dear friends. An ordinary hedge witch, that's me." She leaned in, and her face grew solemn. "But don't let that make you underestimate me. I can be a fierce opponent in battle, as whoever has done this will soon find out."

Looking deep into her eyes, I could absolutely believe she was speaking nothing but the truth.

Taking a deep breath, I nodded. "I don't know how much you know about my family, but I'm the youngest Ravenswind. Amethyst Ravenswind, in fact." I rushed out my name when I finally realized she had given hers, and I hadn't responded with mine. Where were my manners?

Lily smiled at me. "I know quite a bit about your family, dear. I understand the two of us have some things in common."

If she was talking about the absence of magic, wouldn't she be surprised to learn that was no longer the case? At least for now. I hoped to return to that state of being a non-magic witch shortly. Just as soon as we found a way to break my bond with Arc.

Which left an awkward silence. How the heck could I tell this woman that I'd made the son of her favorite family into my familiar? That wasn't likely to go over well. Maybe I'd save that part until I better knew how she'd take it.

"Arc is fine. We're staying at a hotel just outside of town," I said, finally breaking the silence.

She leaned against the sofa and closed her eyes for a few seconds. "Thank the Goddess. We've been so worried. The council is everywhere, and they won't tell us anything. Bloody bureaucrats. Like Arc would have harmed that girl. They'd been best friends their whole lives. In his own way, he loved her."

Lily took a sip of her lemonade and then looked at the glass critically. "Is this a tad too sweet? I'm thinking I may have added a touch too much sugar."

"I think it's perfect the way it is." I paused. "It tastes just like my grandmother made it. You remind me of her, you know."

She smiled at me. "You're not the first to tell me that, actually."

Wait, what? But before I could ask her who that could have been, she was talking again.

"You know, to be honest, I'm not surprised that Sonya was killed. It was bound to happen eventually. The girl was playing with fire."

"Wasn't that her job in a way?" I mean, she did work in demolition. And she was a Fire witch.

Lily laughed. "Not that way, dear. Oh, but that's funny. I must remember that one for Merlin. No, I meant the way she gathered secrets to trade for favors."

"What do you mean?"

She took a deep breath. "I'll give you an example. The first time she found out about me and Merlin, years ago this was, she came to me. She didn't exactly threaten to expose us—like that would have done her any good—but she made it clear that she expected me to give her a favor in return for her silence."

"Sonya tried to blackmail you?"

Her head waggled back and forth. "Blackmail is such a strong word, but yes, in a way, I guess you could call it that."

My brain was going double time. "And this was something she did to others too?"

Lily nodded. "They usually do, don't they? She'd gotten ahead pretty quickly for someone so young. I'm thinking her gathering of secrets had something to do with that."

And just like that, my pool of suspects exploded into being. If only I knew who they were.

"I do, however, so wish the killer hadn't decided to dump the body on poor Arc."

Yeah, me too. I was still reeling from the implications of what she'd told me. Her next question caught me somewhat by surprise.

"So how did you and Arc end up finding each other?" Her eyes widened. "Please tell me the two of you weren't dating."

What would be so bad about that? Did hedge witches have element preferences too? I might not be attracted to Arc in that way, but I take offense that others might not think I'm good enough. It was enough to break through my thought processes.

"We weren't dating. We 'found' each other, as you put it, at the local animal shelter here. He was a cat at the time." I tried to keep the bitterness out of my voice, but I'm not sure how successful I was. It didn't seem to matter to her.

"A cat?" Then she started laughing. "Oh, that smart, smart boy."

Yeah, well, not too smart, if you ask me. He would have been neutered if I hadn't found him when I did. But I wasn't quite willing to go into all of that. Not after her apparent horror at the thought of the two of us dating. Maybe she wasn't nearly as much like my grandmother as I had imagined.

I sat my now empty glass on the table by my chair and stood to leave. "Well, thank you for your time. You've given me a lot to think about." And I headed for the door.

She didn't try to stop me, but she did follow me. "We'll expect the two of you here for a family meeting tonight around seven. We'll eat and then come up with a game plan on how to fix this mess."

Turning to face her, I shook my head. "I don't think that's such a good idea. We've already had one run- in with the council since we got here. They'll be watching us and follow us here. I don't think you want that kind of trouble."

Her eyes flashed. "Let them bring it. I have claws of my own." She paused. "Who exactly did you run into? What happened?"

I shrugged. "I'm not sure. The witch was the ex-wife of Arc's dad, but she didn't seem to be able to recognize Arc in his furry form. Kind of surprised me, actually. I'd thought we were had for sure."

Her expression told me I wasn't the only one surprised by that. But before she could marshal her thoughts for another barrage of questions, I left.

As I climbed into my car, she called out. "See you at seven!"

Yeah, I didn't think that was going to happen.

Chapter 4

When I got back to the hotel, I gave the secret knock before unlocking the door and going in. Arc was feeling pretty on edge ever since running into Patty Bluespring yesterday, and I really didn't want him blasting me.

I found him sitting on the floor beside the second bed at the far end of the room. He would be out of sight there from anyone coming in. Hopefully, for long enough to change.

Once the door was shut and firmly locked with the safety bolt in place, he stood up and stretched. He looked concerned.

"How was Dad?"

"Your father is fine." I hesitated. "I'm guessing you know Lily Hilton?"

"Uncle Merlin's gal? Sure." His eyes lit up. "That's where you should have gone, not the office. Why didn't I think of that?"

"You might not have, but your dad did. That's where he sent me after I met him. She is expecting us for dinner and a family meeting at seven." Or was I just assuming she was offering a meal with it? "I told her I didn't think that was such a good idea."

He grinned at me. "You don't know Lily. It's not a good idea; it's a great idea. That house has so many protection spells and wards on it that a Navy Seals team couldn't break through them." He frowned. "Getting there might be a problem, though."

I really wished I could tell him that if he decided to go, he'd have to go on his own. But that wasn't possible. Lily's home was too far away for four little cat paws, and the man form of Archimedes Mineheart Jr. wasn't safe to be out on the street. Truthfully, I wasn't sure the cat form would be, either, if we ran into a competent council member. I had doubts about Patty's credentials.

But right at that moment, I had more serious matters to discuss with him. Like all the possible new suspects for the murder investigation. I took a minute to brief him. It was still hard for me to believe that he didn't know about her secret gathering if they'd really been as close as he and Lily had thought they were.

"If anyone but Lily had told you that, I'd have called them an outright liar." Then he got quiet and flopped on his back on the bed. "Crap. Now that I think of it, she did that once to me. But I thought she was just joking. I mean, we did favors for each other all the time, and what she was needing at the time wasn't any big deal to me."

"It might have been for her, though."

"Yeah. I'm thinking so, too, now."

"Do you think she kept a list somewhere of her secrets? A place where we could start looking for the nastier ones she was holding over people?"

He shook his head. "I'm fairly sure the police took her home computer. If they didn't, the council did. But Sonya wouldn't keep anything like that on her hard drive. She was too smart for that. If she had a list, it would be on some hidden online account under a false name." He sounded a bit hopeless. "No way to find it on the web."

I wasn't too sure about that. Things like that were my friend Tommy Hill's specialty. Of course, there were a couple of major problems with bringing him into all this. One, he'd already served time for computer hacking and was currently on a short governmental leash. And two, his mother was in jail for trying to kill my aunt Opal, and eventually me too. Her hatred for Opal was just older than her hatred of me, so she'd started with her.

"Are you okay? You don't look so good." I opened my eyes to find Arc hovering over me. When had he gotten up? I'd only lain down for a second. Then I glanced at the clock.

Crap on toast. How could I have fallen asleep with everything that was going on? Then I realized that Arc was still waiting for an answer.

"I'll be okay. All this is just getting to be too much, you know? I mean, I really think the council is playing with us, and I don't like that feeling. If they know you are my cat, then why haven't they pounced on us yet? What are they waiting for?"

He lifted a shoulder. "I'm not so sure they do know I'm the cat. What was it Patty said? Our magical signatures are similar enough to mine to set off the wards, but not identical. They can't really make an arrest without a one hundred percent match."

"But it's you. How can it not be a match?"

He swallowed. "Well, I'm thinking I might owe you more than I thought I did. I think my magical signature changed just a little when you made me your familiar. It makes sense, actually, as much as our magic has blended. Some of your magic must have rubbed off on me, and vice versa."

That might be true if I had any real magic to speak of, but I'd just been using his. Hadn't I?

"I'm sorry I woke you up. You can go back to sleep if you want. We don't have to leave here for another couple of hours."

"Leave? Where . . ." Oh yeah, I still hadn't talked him out of the whole family meeting thing. "Do you really think going to this thing is the smart thing to do? You know the council has to be watching us. Even if we aren't a for sure match, we're close enough that they aren't going to let us very far out of their sight. We're on the radar now. I think our time would be better spent trying to find the killer rather than hanging out with your folks."

Besides, I really didn't want to go. I didn't like the feeling of being thought not good enough for their precious Archimedes Junior.

***

I hated to waste the time just sitting and twiddling my thumbs at the hotel, so I decided to do what I'd intended to finish up today. Check out Firestorm United Demolition. It couldn't hurt, right?

Even if I was sure the killer was most likely on the list of Sonya's secret gathering victims. There was definitely motive to be had there. It was enough to make me question Arc's ability to judge people. It was hard to believe he hadn't had a clue as to that side of her.

I was still wearing my interviewing outfit when I walked into Firestorm's front office. I blame that for the confusion.

The office itself wasn't all that impressive. A small trailer parked outside a much larger warehouse with a sign directing visitors to go there first. No problem. Who knew what they had in that warehouse? Being a demolition company, most likely there were some dangerous things inside. That didn't concern me right now, but it made me nervous at the thought of being so close to a virtual powder keg. I wondered how the neighbors dealt with it on a daily basis.

There was just one man inside the trailer. So much for making friends with a female co-worker and pumping her for information. This was beginning to look like a very small operation.

The man looked up as I entered. The nameplate on his desk said Stan Grayson, not that he bothered to introduce himself. After giving me a onceover, his eyes rested firmly on the area of my breasts. And no, my sweater wasn't that tight. The man was just a chauvinistic pig.

I pasted a fake smile on my face and walked over to his desk. He didn't bother to stand. Another mark not in his favor.

"Oh, please tell me you're here about the job opening," he said with a leer. "If so, you're hired."

Strike three. The man was a class act. I almost walked out, but I didn't. Blackmailer or not, Sonya's murder still deserved justice. And Arc's name still needed to be cleared.

I forced my smile to stay in place. It wasn't easy. "Actually, I was looking for Sonya Ignacio. She works here too, right?"

His face shut down. "Not anymore."

Even after waiting a few seconds, he didn't say anything else. "I see." Ruby would consider that a loss, me talking first. "Can you tell me where she's working now, or how to get ahold of her?"

He took a deep breath and shook his head. "Can't nobody get ahold of her where she's at." Finally, he stood, but only to step around his desk and take my arm to lead me to the door. "Now I think you need to leave."

"What if I've decided the job might be a good fit for me?" I was thinking there was a reason he wanted to be rid of me so quickly, and of course, all that did was make me want to stay and find out what it was.

"The position is no longer available."

With his hand at my back, he literally pushed me out the door and closed it behind me. I heard the lock turn.

Hmm. That was an interesting turn of events.

Maybe the blackmail list didn't hold the only suspects after all. Suddenly, I really wanted Mr. Bigshot to be the killer. The man was a true winner. Women everywhere would be much safer if he were in prison.

I had just reached down to open my car door when I heard him call out behind me. "Wait up!"

What the heck did he want now? I turned to find him walking toward me with a large box. When he reached me, he shoved the box into my arms with such force that I stumbled backward. Luckily, my car helped me stay on my feet.

"You can give Sonya's stuff to your cop buddies. And while you're at it, tell them to lay off me. If they ain't got a brain in their heads between the lot of them, I'll give them a little hint. The one who killed her is Archimedes Mineheart. If it walks like a duck, looks like a duck, and quacks like a duck, then chances are you've got a duck. The same thing goes for killers, too."

He stormed back into his office and slammed the door, not that I had any inclination whatsoever to follow him.

Why look a gift horse in the mouth? Especially, when right at the top of the box sat Sonya's laptop.

My heart was a lot lighter on the way back to the hotel. Not only did we have a whole new avenue to explore via her computer, but we also had a piece of vital and comforting information that we didn't have before.

The police weren't convinced that Arc was the killer. There was hope yet.

Chapter 5

By the time I got back to the hotel, my fingers were itching to try my hand at hacking. If Arc should be wrong about Sonya's intelligence when it came to keeping stuff on her computer, we could have the world of Ignacio at our very fingertips.

It's kind of hard to drive with your fingers crossed, by the way.

I walked into the room to find Arc pacing. That wasn't good. He was losing his fear in all his excitement about seeing his family. If I'd been the council instead of myself, they'd have had him.

"What took you so long? I don't want to be late. Lily really doesn't like it when you show up late. And I know you don't know her, but you really don't want to tick Lily off."

I set the box down on the small room table and hefted out the computer to show Arc. "I don't want to go. I lucked into getting her computer. It was at her office. My time will be better spent here with it."

That derailed him for a minute, at least. "That's Sonya's? And they just gave it to you?"

"Yeah, well, he may have mistakenly believed I was working for the law. And no, I said absolutely nothing to give that impression. He simply jumped to that conclusion because I was asking about Sonya. But here's the best part: the police have been questioning him about her murder. It sounds like they aren't convinced you're the killer. That's great, right?"

He closed his eyes for a few seconds, and his shoulders dropped. Yeah, I'd be saying a thankful prayer to the God and the Goddess too.

"Better than great, actually," he said quietly. Then his eyes flashed to mine. "Now get ready to go. My dad needs to know this."

I just stared at him. "Didn't you hear me? I don't want to go." I hefted the computer and pointed to it.

"Too bad. We're going. You promised to help me, remember? Keeping me cut off from being able to talk with my family isn't helping. I need them." He paused. "They're good, you know. I think they can help us. And the information on that computer has waited this long. It can wait a few more hours."

I wasn't so sure. The whole idea of going to this mini family reunion just seemed like walking into a trap set by the council. Not that his family would be involved in the trap. No, they'd be innocent victims too. In fact, that might be Bluespring's whole reason for not picking us up when she had the chance. Maybe she wanted to wait until she could bring down the whole family on conspirator charges.

That just seemed like something a council member would do. Especially one with a grudge.

Arc didn't think that was the case. "Look, they know by now where we are, and there is absolutely no way they are getting into Lily's house. My family will have taken precautions. We'll be safe there."

I shook my head at him. I really didn't think he was seeing the big picture here. "Was there any way someone could lay a dead body right next to you in your own bed in your own warded apartment without you knowing it?"

He looked hurt. "That was a low blow. I'm still trying to work out how that happened. You're just going to have to trust me that Lily is . . . different. She doesn't take chances. She wouldn't have invited us over if she couldn't handle the possible repercussions."

As much as I hated to even think about it, he wasn't giving me a choice.

We were going.

I still thought that was a very bad idea.

***

It was close, but we were at Lily's door at six o'clock and fifty-nine minutes. A full minute to spare.

Well, I was there. And my little cat too.

She opened the door with a flourish and gathered me into a fierce hug. If anyone was watching, they'd think we were old friends. It was kind of an awkward moment, because as full as my hands were, there was no way I could hug her back. Arc was in one hand in his carrier, and Sonya's computer bag was in the other. I hadn't been willing to leave it behind. It wasn't getting out of my sight until I'd pried all of its secrets out of it.

"Come in, come in. Most everyone is here already." Her voice lowered. "And Merlin can't wait to meet you, dear. He's been waiting such a long time."

Huh? Her words weren't making much sense. After all, they'd only known about me for a few hours. That didn't sound like such a long time to me.

Besides, what had happened to her obvious horror at the idea of Arc and I dating? Things weren't adding up.

The first thing I noticed, other than the two men in the front room, was the delicious smell coming from the kitchen. Memories of my grandmother's house and her full country-cooked meals came flooding back, filling me with a false sense of security. I had to keep reminding myself that I didn't know these people.

Not even Arc, really, even if he was my familiar. It wouldn't do to let my guard down.

"I do hope you like pot roast, dear. Now, everyone go in and get a seat at the table." One of the men followed her command. Arc's dad didn't. He headed straight for the cat carrier.

Bending down, he looked in at Arc. I couldn't see Arc's expression from my height, but I could imagine he wasn't too happy about the situation. Too bad. He was the one who had wanted to come, and this had been the only safe way to do it.

Finally, Senior looked up at me. "I am hoping you remembered to bring clothes for him?"

I nodded and then pulled out the shorts and T-shirt I'd stuffed into the side of the computer bag. Senior took them, opened the carrier, and led Arc to the bathroom. A few minutes later, they both emerged.

Arc looked younger somehow. Then I felt guilty. Of course the man had missed his family. He'd had to do without any of them. At least when my mom went traveling, I still had Opal and Ruby. It must have been terrible being all alone.

Lily shooed me into the kitchen and showed me where to sit. Once everyone was in their places, she introduced me. There was only one person there that I didn't already know. I was guessing that was the uncle, Merlin. I was right.

His smile was warm and welcoming, and I felt my guard slipping just that tiniest of bits. I knew I should be uptight and worried, but this felt . . . odd. How could I feel so at home with these people when I hadn't even known most of them for a full day yet?

After Lily loaded the table down with the food and Merlin said grace, Lily started things off. "First off, there will be absolutely no talk of the awful circumstances Arc has found himself in while we eat. Is that understood?" Her eyes went around the table, waiting until she got a nod from every one of us. "Good. It wouldn't be right to ruin the meal with that kind of talk, and it wouldn't be very nice to get started without our final guest, either."

I glanced around. Who were we missing? Senior wasn't wearing a wedding band, so I'd assumed him to be single, and Merlin's gal was Lily. Was there a cousin or sibling yet to arrive?

It felt too rude of me to ask. Luckily Arc didn't have that problem.

"Who else is coming?" he asked. "The whole family is here already. Is it someone we're sure we can trust?"

"Don't you worry yourself about that, dear," Lily said. "The final guest is your dad's plus one, and absolutely above reproach." Her eyes flashed over to me and then down.

A shiver ran down my spine. I didn't like the fact that they were keeping the identity of the guest a secret. Maybe I'd been lured into a bad situation. What if these people weren't what they seemed?

What if the one yet to come was a council member?

Part of me wanted nothing more than to run. The other, hungrier part of me—the one that had barely had anything to eat all day—wanted pot roast with all the fixings.

Guess which part won?

In the end, I took my cue from Arc. He didn't seem too concerned about it, so I decided I wouldn't be either. Of the two of us, he had more to be worried about, all things considered.

The roast was positively splendid, as were the potatoes and carrots. Absolutely melt-in-your-mouth delicious. I noticed Arc going back for seconds and then thirds. At least I stopped with seconds. It was hard, though.

The talk between the family drifted over me as I ate. They talked about the law firm, cases they were currently working on, basically anything and everything except the one thing everyone most wanted to discuss.

Who the hell had killed Sonya, and why had they decided to try to pin the crime on Arc?

The undercurrent was there, even if we weren't allowed to talk about it. The situation wasn't going to go away or be ignored for long.

When my train of thought finally ran out and I became aware of the conversation again, Arc was asking about a friend of his.

"Has anyone heard from Ryan lately? This must be hitting him hard, losing Sonya and then me disappearing like that."

Merlin shook his head. "Not a peep. Surprising, actually. It seems like everyone else has called. Just not him."

"I really don't see what you all find so likable about that boy," Lily said with a shiver. "The time I met him, he just didn't seem quite right."

Arc nodded. "Yeah, but that was right after he lost his brother. They'd been adopted out to different families, and he'd only found him a couple of weeks before he was killed. Something like that can really mess with your head."

She shook her head. "Maybe." Then she looked up at him with a shrewd look in her eyes. "Didn't he stay with you for a while?"

Arc might not have known what she was saying, but I did. My ears perked up. If he'd stayed with Arc, then he had to have been given a way through the wards.

"Yes. And in case you're wondering, he lost the key to my place the second day."

Merlin almost choked on a bite of roast. "Your warded key?"

Okay, now Arc was fully on board. "Crap. The killer must have found that key."

Perhaps. But how would they have known what it was or who it belonged to? Looked like I would be paying a visit to this Ryan guy. The sooner the better too.

Lily gave Arc a sharp look. "No killer talk at the table, remember?"

I closed my mouth on the words I'd been about to say and ducked my head. When the conversation started up again, it was on a much lighter topic.

We were almost finished when the doorbell rang.

Lily stood and walked out to answer it. I followed. My curiosity was far too great to stay seated. Besides, I wanted to be on my feet in case I'd judged them all wrong and needed to make a break for the back door.

When the door opened and I saw who was standing there, I almost did just that.

Chapter 6

The woman standing on the other side of the threshold was tall, thin, and had a face that I'd seen nearly every day of my life. Aunt Opal. I had no idea how she'd found me, but she had.

Her eyes bypassed Lily and flew straight to me. As I said, the thought of running was a prevalent one. Maybe even the smartest thought I'd had all day. But I didn't run. If she'd found me here, she'd find me wherever I was to run to, too. She had her ways.

"Amethyst Willamina Ravenswind, what in the Goddess's name have you gotten yourself into this time?"

She went to step over the threshold and grunted. Only then did her eyes go to Lily. "That's a powerful ward you have there, ma'am. But I'd appreciate it if you would lift it and allow me to collect my niece. If not, believe me when I say I have other options you might not be so fond of."

Lily stood her ground. If Opal had stopped herself before adding that threat at the end, she might have had better luck. Watching the two of them face off, I had to wonder if just maybe Opal had finally met her match. Funny that it should be in the form of a hedge witch.

"The ward well knows who to let in and who to keep out. If it's keeping you out, then it has a reason. I'll not question that or override it."

Opal's face flushed, and her lips formed a grim smile. "So Archimedes Mineheart Jr. is in this house, then." She didn't make it a question. "You do realize that by harboring a witch wanted by the council, you are in essence breaking the witches' creed."

"I'd like to hear just how my protecting an innocent man from being persecuted by the council is harming anyone, Opal Ravenswind." Her eyes darkened. "If anyone is breaking the creed, it's you and the bloody council on this one."

Opal's eyes reluctantly left those of the woman in front of her. She wasn't one to break eye contact in a battle lightly. When they focused back on me, I had to swallow. Opal had another priority that night higher than the one of bringing in Arc. She wasn't there for him. She was there for me.

I stepped forward, but not enough for her to reach me without crossing the threshold. I'm not that stupid.

"I'm afraid Lily is right, Opal. I know you are honor bound to do the council's bidding, but they're wrong on this one. Arc didn't kill Sonya. Just ask Ruby."

Her eyes flashed. "You've brought my daughter into this mess?"

Another swallow. "In my defense, I didn't know what the mess was at the time. By the time we knew, then yes, she was in on the secret."

"How?"

"I needed her to do a truth spell on Arc . . . Archimedes, that is. She did, and he still said he didn't do it. He's innocent, Opal. The council has its sights on the wrong man."

Opal grimaced and shook her head. "You ignorant little witch. Earth witches don't think much of us Air witches. Most likely he has some sort of personal ward to keep our magic from affecting him."

"Well, if that was the case, then how the bloody heck did I manage to do the binding spell to make him my familiar?"

"What?" It wasn't just one voice that spoke that word, but three. Lily, Senior, and Merlin. I glanced at them and lifted a shoulder.

I would have to deal with them later. Or even better, Arc could do it. That situation was every bit as much his fault as mine.

The biggest threat to my personal wellbeing was standing on the other side of that well-guarded threshold. That was what I needed to defuse first.

When I glanced back at my aunt, it surprised me to find her with a smug smile on her face. "Seems I'm not the last one to know everything after all."

Then she turned to Lily. "I apologize for my earlier aggression. Might I enter under a witch's truce?"

Lily glanced back at me. Like I was brave enough to say no. I was living in the woman's house. I couldn't avoid her forever.

Finally, she nodded, chanted a short incantation, and stepped back. Opal was in.

"Seeing as how we are all now honor bound to the terms of a witch's truce," Lily started, "if you're hungry, there is still some pot roast left. That is, if Arc hasn't already devoured the last of it."

To my surprise, Opal nodded. "That sounds lovely. And perhaps while I eat, I might have a word alone with my niece?"

Ah, there it was. The hidden sting I'd been worried about. The last thing I wanted was to be alone with Opal right now. I needed witnesses, dang it. But Lily had already agreed.

"I'll get you a plate, and the two of you can eat out on the back deck. Plenty of privacy there. I guarantee it."

Opal gave her a half smile. "I don't doubt your abilities one little bit, Ms. . . . . I'm sorry. I seem to have forgotten the introduction part. Obviously you know who I am, but I'm afraid I don't have the same convenience."

"I'm Lily Hilton." She nodded over at the men in attendance. "The ones standing together are the two Archimedes, Senior and Junior. The one on the left is Merlin, Senior's brother."

"I wish I could say it was a pleasure, but under the circumstances, I just can't bring myself to tell that big of a whopper."

Lily laughed. "I appreciate the honesty. I think this evening will be a good one for that."

After the plate was filled and Opal and I had stepped out onto the back patio, the real fun began. It surprised me when my aunt took a bite before beginning the interrogation. Hopefully, the delicious food would be a factor in my favor. If anything could mellow my aunt, it was good food. Too bad I didn't have any raspberry donuts handy.

After she had carefully chewed and swallowed, her eyes locked onto me. "Start from the beginning and leave nothing out."

"Before I do, Opal, I have to know one thing. How did you find me? Or was it Arc you found?"

She grunted. "I got a phone call from Patricia Bluespring. After a few minutes on the phone with her, I started seeing things I'd missed before." Her eyes literally sparked at me. "You had that man upstairs the whole time, didn't you?"

"Well, in the beginning, I didn't exactly know he was a man . . ." There really wasn't any reason left to hide anything. The truth was, if she hadn't been dealing with her own crisis, she'd have found me out far sooner.

But then again, if it hadn't been for her being the lead suspect in a murder investigation when the rest of my family were away, I wouldn't have been looking for a familiar in the first place. In a way, this was on her. Not that I could ever tell her that.

"Does she know?"

Opal barked out a laugh. "Patricia? Goddess, no. Who in their right mind would think one witch would have the audacity to make another, even more powerful witch her familiar? She doesn't have a clue."

"And you came to me first." I had to swallow hard. "Thank you."

Her hand reached over and grabbed mine. "It's true I'm honor bound to the council, and that's something I don't take lightly. Like it or not, what we do is important in keeping things safe for all of us. We don't want the witch hunts to start again, and you get rogue witches using magic for evil purposes, and it's only a matter of time." Then her hand squeezed mine. "But family comes first, child. Always has, always will."

In the next five minutes, I told her everything. Right from the beginning. Her eyes widened when I told her about growing a mature oak tree in a matter of seconds, but she didn't say a word. Not even after I'd finished.

Taking the last bite, she chewed thoughtfully. I was trying really hard to follow Ruby's advice and not be the first one to speak, but I was up against a master of the art. Ruby's Obi-Wan.

"I've really screwed up, haven't I?"

Opal took a deep breath and nodded. "Yes, you have. But for what it is worth, your intentions were good, child. And, as much as I hate to admit it, bringing Ruby in for that truth spell was a stroke of pure genius. Not sure I'd have thought of that, being in your shoes."

A compliment from Opal?

"Of course, you know what they say about good intentions. They pave the road to hell with 'em. That could likely be the case here." She paused, pursing her lips and gazing up into the night sky. No full moon tonight. "Don't suppose you'd listen to reason and come home with me? Let the Earth witches figure out their own mess?"

"I owe him, Opal. And one thing you and Mom always taught us was to pay our debts."

"Yes, well, there are exceptions to every rule. Even that one. But this might not be one of them." She took another swig of Lily's awesome lemonade. "Remind me to get her recipe for this. I can never get mine to taste this good."

"Can I ask you something, Opal?" Something had been weighing heavily on my mind for quite a while. Might as well ask it now while Opal was actually being approachable. That wasn't likely to last for long.

"You want to know why your magical signature is so close to Archimedes', don't you?"

I'll never be fully convinced she can't read my mind. But it saved me from having to form the words. I just went with a nod.

She shook her head. "I wish I knew, child. That's the one thing that's bothered me most in all this. I realized the similarities right from the beginning. They weren't as strong then, because you hadn't really come into your magic, but they were there. Now . . . you're almost a match for him. And I don't have a clue how that could be."

"Maybe I can shed some light on that for you."

Wait, I knew that voice.

Opal and I whirled around to find Mom standing right behind us, the door leading back into the house still open.

What the hell was she doing here?

And more importantly, what light?

Chapter 7

Opal wasn't happy when Mom insisted that we go back inside to continue our family reunion. But, like me, she was far too curious not to follow her, anyway. I could only wonder if she had the same feeling I did.

That all of our lives were about to change.

Arc and his family were still seated at the table, but the food had been put away. It was a good thing Lily had a big table for eight. We even had a chair to spare.

Mom looked at the chair with a bit of sadness. "I really wish Ruby were here for this, but there is no helping it at this point. The time has come."

She was sitting directly to the left of Senior, which I thought was a little odd. At least, I thought it was odd until she reached over and they grasped each other's hands. The look she gave him sent chills down my spine. I'd been right. Whatever was coming would be life-changing information.

"You are going to probably be upset that we have kept this from the two of you for so long, but I'm a firm believer that the Universe, Fate, or whatever you want to call it, would be a better judge of when the right time of illumination would be than I would be." She smiled at me and Arc in turn. "And it would seem the Universe has spoken in a very resounding voice."

That's when the butterflies in my stomach kicked in. A quick glance at Arc showed me that he was just as clueless as I was. That was something, anyway.

"Oh, Sapphire, you didn't! With an Earth witch?" That was Opal. She must have the same mind-reading ability with Mom that she had with me. That, or I was just a tad bit slow with hints and clues. Not a good thing for a wannabe detective.

Mom raised her head a little higher. "That kind of prejudice is exactly why this news has taken this long to reveal itself. And why I felt the need to hide it from you." Mom's eyes sought out mine, and they looked sad. "I have a confession, love. I haven't been traveling the world. Archie and I have been back from our honeymoon for weeks now."

"You're married?" And more importantly, I wasn't invited?

She must have just realized that little fact would probably get my attention in the wrong way. "I wanted you there, love, but—"

"But I've always been able to read you like a book. If you knew, then I'd know," Opal said, giving Mom one of her signature looks. "But this isn't the news you have to share, is it?"

Mom shook her head. "A part of it, but no, not the most important part."

I wasn't getting it, even if Aunt Opal was already on board. What could possibly be more important news than the fact that Archimedes Mineheart Sr. was now my stepfather?

"Arc, Amie, obviously you know now that your magical signatures are practically the same. Part of that is because of the familiar binding—which I totally want to hear all about, by the way—but another part, the foundational part, is because you two are family."

It took Arc's horrified look to get me on board. Here I was still thinking she meant in a step-family kind of way. His look said otherwise.

Then I remembered Lily's horror at the thought of the two of us dating. Oh my Goddess, no. She wouldn't keep something like that from me all my life. Would she?

Mom shoved a paper bag across the table to me. In times like this, I tended to hyperventilate. In times of real crises, I was fine. But if there wasn't any immediate danger, then my emotions could get the better of me in a heartbeat.

I started breathing into the bag. It helped, but my heart and mind wouldn't stop racing. Both down the same track.

Arc was my brother.

I had a brother.

***

After the bombshell that Mom dropped on us, it took a while to get my breathing under control. Once I did, I left. Arc stayed behind, now a guest of Lily's. She'd offered me her second guestroom, but I wasn't exactly in the mood for company. Even if there was a door between us.

I needed to be alone. Or better yet, with Ruby. I decided that I needed to be the one to tell her. Not Mom, not Opal, me. The only bad part was that I didn't have it in me to make that long of a drive. I was kind of amazed I'd made it to the hotel in one piece, actually.

Once inside, I speed dialed Ruby's cell phone.

"Hey, Ams, what's up?" Then a few seconds of silence. Guess I should have marshaled my thoughts together before dialing. "Oh no, Mom's there, isn't she? What has she done?"

"It's not Opal. Well, I mean, yes, she's here, but she isn't why I'm calling. Mom's here too." And once again, my verbal well ran dry.

"Sapphire's there? How? When did she get in? Is she okay?"

My brain was still whirling. Maybe calling Ruby this soon hadn't been such a great idea after all.

"Amie? Are you okay?"

"Yeah, it's just . . ." There just wasn't an easy way to do this. "Arc and I are brother and sister, Ruby. We're related."

Now the silence was coming from her end. It must be catching.

"I'm coming. You're still at the Oak Hill Lodge, right?"

"Yeah, but it's just me for now. Arc stayed at . . . friends. We both need some time to think this through." Then I glanced at the clock. It was almost eleven. Far too late for Ruby to try to make it here tonight, as much as I wanted her to. "Look, now that I think about it, I probably shouldn't have called you with this. I was just in shock, and, well, I wanted you to hear it from me."

"You'd better be glad you did call, missy." Missy? She was a whole two minutes older than me.

"Yeah, well, please don't do anything rash. Truthfully, I think your mom might need you more tonight than I do. She looked pretty shaken."

More silence. Once again, I lost.

"Don't come tonight, okay? It's too late to try to get a ride, and I'm pretty wiped out after the day I've had.

Maybe Opal can bring you down tomorrow night after the shop closes?"

"You sure you're okay to be by yourself tonight?" Her voice was soft. I knew she had to be torn between me and Opal. I was trying to make it easier for her, dang it.

"I'll be fine. I mean, hey, I have a brother, right? Isn't that something both of us always wished we'd had?"

She gave a dry laugh. "We had Opie. That's every bit as good." Then she must have realized that it wasn't such a good idea bringing him up at a time like this. Not when I was already hurting from his absence. "Sorry, Amie. I shouldn't have brought him up."

"It's okay. I do miss him, though." I had to get off the phone soon. If I started crying, there was no way in heck she wouldn't find her way here tonight. And suddenly, I really did just want to be alone.

Besides, I had Sonya's computer to crack.

Hopefully, that would distract me from the emotional turmoil my body was reeling with right now. And maybe even help us catch the killer so we could get our lives back to normal.

Whatever the new normal was.

Chapter 8

It didn't really matter how long I stared at the computer's login screen. The password wasn't going to magically appear. Technology might seem like magic, but it wasn't. In fact, the two didn't play well with each other at all.

Even if I had the control I should have on my new abilities, I'd be afraid to spell the computer. For one, it was the laptop of a witch and was most likely warded for that. Especially seeing as the side business Sonya was doing wasn't exactly on the legal up and up. For another, with my habit of overdoing things, if I could get the spell to work, it would probably wipe out the hard drive.

I stared a little longer, but no new ideas came to me. There was no way I was getting this done on my own. I needed help.

I needed the hot geek. Of course, getting his help might have been a lot easier before slamming his mom into a wall last week with my new found power. But then, she had been trying to kill my aunt and cousin at the time, so at least it had been justified.

Besides, what choice did I have? I needed to know what was on this thing, and the little flashing cursor was just sitting there mocking me.

A call wouldn't work, either. If Tommy really did get out of prison on a super-secret government hacking gig parole, his phone lines would be being watched. Or, more to the point, listened in to. I'd have to make a drive back to Wind's Crossing.

Surely they weren't actually watching his place twenty-four hours a day. Even if they were, well, who was to say I wasn't there for a booty call? It wasn't like the attraction wasn't there. It was. It was just super complicated.

The drive took a full hour. I wasn't pushing things. The very last thing I needed right now was a moving violation. My bills were racking up as it was, and those things weren't cheap.

By the time I pulled up outside Tommy's new loft apartment, it was going on one o'clock in the morning. The absence of light told me that Tommy was likely fast asleep. Just like I should be.

Taking a deep breath, I opened the car door, stepped out, and lugged the computer case up the steps to Tommy's door. It took a couple of minutes before he finally answered.

Dang. My friend Opie had a six-pack too, but Tommy's had a little added muscle. I knew this because Tommy wasn't wearing a shirt. Or long pants. In fact, he had on the cutest little pajama shorts I'd ever seen. Emphasis on the little.

I'd be lying if I said he wasn't surprised to see me standing there right on his landing.

He blinked at me a couple of times. Like I would disappear or something.

"Hey, Tommy. I'm sorry I woke you up, but I could really use your help with something." I hefted the laptop case so he'd get the hint.

He sucked in some air and bit his lower lip. We must have stood like that for a full minute before he finally said. "Sure, Amie, I can help you with that." He lowered his voice. "Not here. Give me a minute to get dressed, and I'll meet you down below."

He was even faster at dressing than Opie. It was only seconds later that he came out of his door. Of course, it doesn't take all that long to throw on a T-shirt and step into flip-flops.

When he reached me, he said, "Let's walk."

We waited until we were a good half block away before either of us said anything.

"They really do have you on a short leash, don't they?"

Tommy made a face. "You have no idea." He glanced down at the laptop bag. "I can't touch that, you know. They make me take lie detector tests sometimes." He shivered. "I really don't want to go back to prison. And if I get caught, it'll be a longer sentence. They made that abundantly clear."

Now I was feeling guilty about coming. Who was I to put his freedom in jeopardy?

"I shouldn't have come." I started to turn around, but he reached out a hand and stopped me.

"I didn't say I wouldn't help you. I just can't do the actual work. You'll have to."

Still sounded risky to me. What if they asked just the right question when he was all hooked up? That didn't change the fact that I needed help. And he was the smartest person with computers that I knew. I mean, he had to be if the government drafted him from prison, right?

"What if I told you that I got a computer from a friend's estate and that all I needed was the password to get into it? The . . . estate didn't know it." I spoke slowly, trying to come up with a plausible story that might not get him into trouble with the Feds. "I'd really like to be able to access the computer because I know my friend kept a lot of photographs and stuff on the computer, and I'd love to have them."

Kind of sort of the truth. In part, anyway. Sonya wasn't exactly a friend, as I'd never even met her. Did friend of my new found brother count for anything?

He thought about it and then nodded slowly. "I can work with that." He paused. "Do you have a paper and pen?"

After a brief ramble inside my purse, I came up with the back of an envelope and a mechanical pencil. Close enough.

"Okay, the first thing you do is get a USB drive. Then you download this software from another computer onto the drive." He scribbled briefly on the back of the envelope. "Once you've done that, search the internet for this software, and you'll find some videos that will show you exactly how to do it. If you even need them. It's really simple. Once you have the software on the drive, you basically just plug it into the estate laptop and then do a reboot. The instructions will pop up from there for you to reset the password."

He was stepping a lot lighter now. I think he was relieved that I hadn't asked him to do any major hacking. That hadn't been the plan tonight, but depending on what the computer gave up in the way of files, I still might need that. I'd just have to find some other way to get it.

"What do you know? I was able to help you and keep my word to the Feds, too. All I did was give you the name of a software to reset your password. What could the harm in that be?"

I bit my tongue and smiled at him. He didn't need to know that technically the laptop should be in the possession of the police instead of me.

"Thank you, Tommy. This helps a lot." We turned the corner of our around the block walk and started back toward his loft. I didn't say what I really wanted to. We both knew that if it had come right down to it, Tommy would have helped me. No matter what I'd asked. He was a good friend. A better one than me, obviously.

He shrugged. "I owe you. Especially after the whole my mom trying to kill your whole family thing."

We walked a few more steps in silence.

"There's no way for us to get past that, is there?"

I knew what he meant, even if he wasn't spelling it all out. He wondered if there was still a chance between us.

The question deserved some thought, so I took a minute. Finally, I shook my head. "I really don't think there is, Tommy. Let's face it, right now your mom is hanging by a really slim thread. If we got together as a couple, I think that thread would snap."

He blew out a breath. "Yeah, that's what I think too." Then he gave me a sad smile. "It's too bad, though. I really think we would have been great together. Now we'll never know."

I blinked the sudden moisture out of my eyes. What was it with me losing the men in my life lately? Not lovers, but friends. Somehow, that only seemed to make it worse. I didn't want to lose Tommy. But was it fair to keep him locked into friendship when he wanted more?

"I think maybe you're right. You're a hell of a guy, Tommy Hill. And just so you know, you'll never be Fat Geek again. You're Hot Geek now."

He gave a little laugh. "Hot Geek, huh? I think I like the sound of that."

We reached the bottom of his stairs, and I stood on tippy-toe to brush my lips against his. "Goodbye, Tommy."

He pulled me in for a hug, and we stood there in the light of the moon for several seconds before he finally whispered, "Goodbye, Amie."

Then he walked up the stairs and went inside without ever looking back. I got into my car and drove a couple blocks before having to pull over.

It was hard to drive when you couldn't see the road through your tears.

Chapter 9

I'm not sure how I made it back to the hotel, but I did. I'd been tempted to head for the farmhouse, but that wouldn't have been fair to Opal and Ruby. They had day jobs at the shop. They needed their sleep.

Apparently, even in the midst of all of this, so did I. I woke up at nine in the morning, still fully dressed, on the hotel bed. After dealing with the whole where the heck am I thing of waking in a strange bed, I used the bathroom and then popped open the computer.

I was lucky enough to already have a USB drive, so I started right in. Tommy was right. It was easy. Which was scary in a way, but good for me now. Within a half hour, I was in and with full administrative power too. That meant that the computer files were fully visible and accessible. Go me.

The first thing I did was take a really close look at her desktop. Then I found myself staring. Arc had thought she was computer smart. But then, Arc had thought a lot of things about Sonya that had turned out to not be true. This just might be another of them.

Because right there on her desktop was a little file icon titled Online PWs. If PW meant to her what it meant to me, my job today would be an easy one. No Tommy Hill required. Which was good, because after last night, no way was I bringing him into this again. There was just too much risk involved.

A quick click and a file opened, listing about fifteen different website accounts, complete with login IDs and passwords. I considered calling Arc, but he had made his choice last night to stay with Lily. Not that I blamed him. Even with the locks and quickie wards we'd done here, our room could probably be breached by a persistent girl scout selling cookies. Lily's home had kept out Opal.

Now that was safety. Though I wondered what protection she had against fire. I mean, just because someone couldn't get in didn't mean they couldn't smoke out the ones inside, right? But then again, from what little I knew of the Minehearts and Lily, they'd probably taken care of that risk too.

When this was all said and done, I'd have to ask them to do the same for the farmhouse. A witch couldn't be too careful in these troubling times. Heck, no one could. They would probably make more money if they gave up their legal trade and focused on home security.

Then again, people would have to embrace magic and come to terms with its existence. That wasn't likely to happen anytime soon.

I glanced down the list and found an online journal. That looked like a good one to start with. In under a minute, I was logged into Sonya's account. Bingo. Within the account were a multitude of files, but one stood out from the rest. It was just titled Ledger.

Another click and a list about a page long appeared. There were three columns. The headers included: name, secret, and payment required.

It was eye-opening. Thirty people were listed. Some of the secrets weren't all that impressive, but then, neither were the payments she wanted out of them. One was as simple as an invitation to a party. The secret for that one was that the woman had lied on her job application by overstating her education.

I pulled a notebook over and started writing down the more interesting of them. As far as I could tell, there were three main suspects. They were the only ones with secrets that seemed to be worth killing for.

What was it the television cop shows always said about motive? Love, money, or revenge, right? Taking the risk of killing someone just so your neighbor doesn't find out you were the one letting your dog poop in their yard just didn't feel right. Too much risk for just having to deal with an angry neighbor . . . and pick up a little doggie doo.

The three I had, though, were real possibilities. A prim and proper grade school librarian who had a sexy peep show on the internet bringing her in an extra income. A local businessman who had been involved in a hit-and-run that resulted in serious injury—the victim was still in a coma in the hospital. And last, a mother with three children. Her secret? Her youngest wasn't her husband's child.

I could see any of those three being willing to kill Sonya to keep their secret from getting out. That wasn't the problem.

The problem was that I couldn't see them taking the next step and trying to blame it on Arc. What possible motive could they have had for that?

Regardless, they were definitely worth checking out. With any luck, I could do it all in one day. Then, after making sure the computer didn't hold any other secrets, we'd make sure it got to where it belonged.

The police. That should help to strengthen their belief that maybe, just maybe, Arc wasn't the killer after all.

***

With a plan for the day, I took a quick shower and got dressed in black jeans and a black sweatshirt. What Ruby called my cat burglar outfit. Not that being dressed all in black would help me out in broad daylight, but still, the outfit made me feel just a little bit badass.

I needed that today.

My only hesitation was in leaving the computer here while I went. It was now a pretty important piece of evidence that might go a long way in proving Arc's innocence. And who was to say that the council might not break in while the room was empty and take it? As convinced as they were—except maybe Opal now—they might be tempted to destroy evidence that countered that belief.

Especially if the council sneak thief happened to be Patricia Bluespring.

Better to take it with me. It wasn't hot enough that being locked in the car's trunk should damage it. I stepped out into the warm spring sunshine and almost dropped the bag.

Right there, parked directly in front of my hotel room door, was Opie's car. And Opie was there too, leaning on the hood, staring at my room, and now me.

I was speechless. And no, that wasn't like me.

"Hey," he said. "Is this a bad time?"

I shook my head. Part of me wanted nothing more than to set the bag down and pounce on him. But another part was still hurting a little too badly from his sudden and thorough disappearance after my magic act.

"I can spare a few minutes. You want to go inside?"

He smiled and nodded. Then stood up and hefted the white bag that had been sitting by him. "I brought breakfast."

I recognized that bag. He'd brought Flour Pot donuts. Maybe there was hope for the two of us yet.

"What about the coffee?" Or better yet, latte, but right now, I wasn't going to be choosy.

"Sorry, I drank mine on the way, and I didn't think a latte would survive the drive and still be drinkable. I did see a coffee pot in the hotel office."

It wouldn't be Flour Pot coffee, but it would have to do. We walked down together and grabbed a cup each and then made our way back to the room.

Once inside, his eyes widened. "You know, this isn't half bad. I'll admit, the outside had me worried."

"Yeah. Best kept secret in town. The Lodge is actually worth twice the price they charge to stay here. Opal would give a lot to have some of this furniture in that shop of hers."

His hand ran over one of the nightstands, and he smiled. "Something like this would totally dress up my bedroom too."

I put my coffee cup down on the tiny table and sat in one of its two chairs. After a second's hesitation, Opie did the same.

Grabbing a donut, I started munching. It had been a while since I'd stuffed myself with pot roast. Besides, no way was I losing this one. He was going to go first. He's the one who left.

"I've been a jerk, haven't I?"

I licked the excess sugar off my lips and considered for a minute. "I'd like to say yes, but I don't really think that's true. Even though it feels a little bit like you were." I hesitated and my voice lowered. "I had to have scared the hell out of you that day, but the truth is, after it was all over with? I was pretty damned scared myself. I could have used you there."

He winced. "I know. It wasn't cool, me dissing you like that. It's just . . . all those years you and Ruby talked about being witches and magic and stuff, and I just thought—okay, they're eccentric. I never really believed it was all real. Then I saw that light when you guys set up that ward on the farmhouse, and I thought—okay, so this is kind of cool."

Opie swallowed, his fingers tracing the outside of the napkin his untouched donut sat on. His eyes never once looked into mine. For Opie, the untouched donut kind of said it all.

"What happened that day at Opal's shop? That wasn't so cool."

Now it was my turn to swallow. He was right. I'd let my anger get the better of me. I'd have killed Naomi Hill if Opal hadn't stopped me. And we both knew it.

"I know. Remember me and Ruby talking about how she had magic, and I didn't?"

He barked out a laugh. "Yeah, well, that was a lie." He sounded hurt.

"No, it wasn't. That night you came to Ruby and me in the park? That was the night I . . ." Just how much did I want to involve Opie in all of this? He was a sheriff's deputy after all. But then again, he was also my best friend who wasn't blood related. "That was the night I got my familiar. And my magic."

His eyes finally met mine. "You really didn't have magic before then?"

I shook my head. "Not an ounce, really. I'd always thought Ruby got it all when she came out two minutes ahead of me. I think that's part of why I fainted that night. Doing magic for the first time is more than a little scary." Especially with the kind of power I'd wielded that night.

"All your life you had no magic, and now, suddenly, you have this kind of power?"

"Yeah. But as you could see, I don't really have any control over it. Not yet. I'm looking for a way to break the familiar spell. Then I can go back to being magic-less Amie." And maybe you'll like me again. But I kept that last part to myself.

"Is that what you really want?"

I shrugged. "If it's either that or become the crazy witch I was back at Opal's shop, then yes. That's what I want."

"Is it that hard to break the spell?"

"Without hurting the familiar, it would seem so." And hurting the familiar wasn't an option in my case.

He blew out a breath. "Okay, so right now you're in limbo. I get that." He glanced around the hotel room. "Is there a reason why you're spending your limbo here rather than at home?"

"I'm working a job."

His eyes flashed back to me. "What kind of job?"

Either way I answered, he wouldn't be happy. He didn't like either of my new lines of work. One I wasn't even qualified to practice yet.

"It's an investigation." He started to speak, but I put a finger on his lips. My touch seemed to shock him, and I'd admit I felt a little electrical current pass between us

69

too. But the important thing was it stopped him from talking. Now if I could just remember what it was I was going to say.

Oh yeah, the investigation thing. "It's not a paid job, so it's legal for me to be asking questions and doing my thing." I paused. "It's another family thing." Even if I hadn't known that when it started.

Opie groaned. "Oh Lord, I turn my back on you gals for a few days, and you manage to find even more trouble. What is it now? Who's in trouble?"

Funny, but I didn't think he'd be all that receptive to the fact that I was trying to clear my brother's name. Especially since Opie and I had been friends practically all our lives, and no brother had ever put in an appearance. Until now.

"It's a long story, but I'm looking into the Sonya Ignacio murder."

His face instantly went blank even as his back straightened in the chair across from me. "They know who did that. Archimedes Mineheart. And I don't want you going anywhere near that man. He's a very bad man, Amie."

Which of course was when the not so bad very bad man decided to show up.

Bad timing must run in the family.

Chapter 10

At the farmhouse, I would have been alerted to the company by the sound of tires on gravel. Here at the hotel, I wasn't afforded that warning. Cars were coming and going all the time. I blame that for what happened next.

The door opened and there stood Arc in all his glory, wearing just a pair of shorts. Most likely he'd made the journey as a cat, but then again, maybe not. He was getting bolder about taking risks of being seen, and that had me worried.

Especially since the first thing Opie did when he walked in was tackle him to the ground. Once he had him face down on the floor, he pulled out his cell phone. Luckily, I got it out of his hand before he could speed dial his dad. Not that his dad would have any kind of jurisdiction here, but he would for sure know who to call that did.

"Amie, give me my phone. Or call nine-one-one yourself." Opie was sweating, and I could see a little tinge of red showing through his pants. He must have torn something loose doing that flying tackle.

"Opie, get off him. You're bleeding."

As I'd expected, Opie totally ignored me. "Archimedes Mineheart, I am hereby arresting you on suspicion of—"

"Oh, for the God and Goddess's sake, Opie, get off that poor boy."

Opie's head snapped around to find my mom standing in the doorway. She came in and firmly shut the door behind her. "Arc didn't kill that girl any more than I did. Now get up."

He wasn't happy about it, but what could he do? We outnumbered him two to one. Three to one if you counted the witch he was currently sitting on.

Standing up, he winced and glanced down at his leg. It had to hurt.

"Lie down on the bed and let me take a look at that leg. That's where you got shot, isn't it?" Mom, bless her heart, was going into full-on mother mode.

Opie looked at her and then at me, but with quick glances. Arc was always in his sight, at least in his peripheral vision. "Would someone mind telling me just what the . . . heck is going on here? This man"—he pointed at Arc—"is wanted for murder. He's dangerous."

"Oh, he is not, dear," Mom said. "Dangerous, I mean. Yes, he's wanted for questioning in Sonya's death, but he isn't guilty, and we're doing our best to prove that." Then she got that steely, no-nonsense look in her eyes. "Now, lie down so I can take a look at your leg."

"I'm not lying down while he's still just standing there free."

I glanced at Arc. He looked concerned and was rubbing his elbow. Most likely he'd have a major carpet burn out of all this. Served him right for taking chances. Maybe now he'd be more careful about showing himself around town. One slip in view of the council and we'd all be in deep ca-ca.

"Oh, for goodness' sake," I said. "Arc, sit down over on your bed where Opie can see you and be between you and the door. I think that'll make him happy."

"His bed?" Opie's voice sounded more than a little strangled.

"Well, my budget didn't have the means to support separate rooms, so yes, his bed."

"Don't worry, Opie, Amie and Arc aren't in any kind of dating relationship. In fact, they're family."

Opie watched Arc walk around him, giving him plenty of room, and then sit on the other bed. Once Arc was down, Opie stretched out with his back to the headboard so that Mom could pull up his pants leg far enough to see the damage. At least, she tried.

"You'll have to take the pants off, dear."

He looked at her and then me. "Not happening, Ms. Ravenswind."

"Oh, for the love of Pete," I said. I grabbed Arc's hand and pulled him into the small bathroom with me. "Call us when you're done."

Mom was the best healer of all us Ravenswinds, so it didn't take long. Within ten minutes, we were back in the main hotel room. Good thing, too. The tiny bathroom really wasn't meant to hold two people at a time. Especially when one of them was a little freaked out. And it wasn't me this time.

By the time we all rejoined, both Arc and Opie were a little calmer. I'd tried to talk Arc down, and it was kind of obvious that Mom had helped Opie with a touch of magic. He seemed a lot more mellow now.

At least he wasn't trying to tackle Arc anymore. That was a big improvement right there.

"How are you doing?" I asked Opie. I felt bad that he'd gotten hurt. Most likely his primary mission in taking

Arc down was to protect me. He was like that. My own personal knight in dented armor.

He gave me a lopsided smile. "Better. Those pills your mom gave me really work fast."

Mom and I shared a quick glance. Yeah sure, it was the pills. But if it helped him to think so, that was okay by us.

"It wasn't too bad. I was able to fix him up pretty good," Mom said. "He should be fine as long as he doesn't make any sudden movements for a while. Wounds like that take time to heal. You're on medical leave for a reason, Opie."

He was on medical leave? That made sense. Now that I thought about it, this wasn't his normal day off.

"How long are you off work?" I felt guilty about asking, but a little help with the investigation from someone who actually knew what they were doing would be great. If he would agree to help out a really bad man like Arc. Maybe I'd get lucky and he'd do it for me.

"I go back one week from today." Then he made a face. "To desk duty until I'm fully released by the medical staff. Hopefully that will be real soon. I hate desk work."

Most cops did, it seemed.

I glanced over at Arc. "Are you still going to stay at . . . your friends?" No sense giving Opie too much information until we saw whether or not he was going to join our side.

Arc nodded. "I just came for my bag and stuff." He looked deep into my eyes. "I really appreciate all you've done for me, Amie. If it hadn't been for you, I'd be in the council's hands right now. Thanks."

Then he grabbed the few toiletries he had out, shoved them into his bag, and he and Mom left. Back to just the two of us. Me and my best pal Opie.

After locking the door, I laid down beside Opie on the bed. He scooted down from the headboard so that we were lying side by side. I put one hand over onto his rock-solid chest.

"I've missed you."

"Ditto."

We laid in silence like that for a while, just reveling in the fact that we were together again. You might not think a few days would hurt as much as it had. But then, you didn't know me and Opie. In a lot of ways, we were closer than family. He chose to be with me, whereas my family just kind of got stuck with me. That meant something.

"I can't believe I'm going to ask this, but why are you so sure Archimedes is innocent?"

I took a deep breath. He might not like the answer, but he deserved the truth. All of it. "I had Ruby do a truth spell on him. Trust me, it works better than one of your lie detector tests. And he said he didn't do it." I rubbed my hand over his chest, soaking in the sheer strength of the man. "Plus, how stupid would you have to be to kill a woman and then put her in your bed? Arc said there wasn't a noticeable amount of blood anywhere in his apartment that he could see. Why kill her and bring her home for the police to find? And speaking of that, how did the cops even know to come barreling in like that? With a trinity of witches' council members, no less. Answer: the killer tipped them off."

Opie grunted. "Okay, I'll give you that." Another minute of silence. I was considering unbuttoning his shirt to get at his skin, when he spoke again. "I'm not going to be able to talk you out of this, am I?"

"Nope." I hesitated, then just told him the rest of the story. He deserved to know, and it should come from me.

I could tell he didn't want to believe me at first. But eventually, his body relaxed again. "He's really your brother? No kidding here?"

"Yup. Well, half-brother. I guess his dad sowed some wild oats when he was younger. Arc was one of them, and I was another. Now he and Mom are actually married. I'm still kind of pissed about not being invited to the wedding."

"No doubt."

The next silence was longer. So long in fact that I fell asleep. It had been a long, hard night, and I'd only gotten a few hours of rest before getting up to tackle the whole computer thing. Plus, it felt really good lying there next to Opie. I was safe. He would make sure of that.

Chapter 11

When I woke up, he was gone. Well, from the bed. I looked over, and he was sitting at the table with Sonya's laptop open, going through my notes.

I sat up and stretched. I could get used to waking up with him there. It was sure a better feeling than the last few days without him had brought me.

"Good, you're awake." He pointed to the computer in front of him. "I think you might be right about Arc's innocence after all."

Well, yeah. Did he miss the whole part about the truth spell, or what?

"What brought you over to our side?"

"Well, first of all, this Sonya chick wasn't a nice lady. At all. Any number of people on this ledger would have reason to do her in. And yes, I've seen your notes, and for the most part, I agree with them. Those three would be my top picks for suspects too."

"But . . ."

"But you can't really stop there. People are strange creatures. For some, it would take an unbelievable amount of motivation to kill someone. Like, say, the person shot their dog or something." Yeah, yet another reference to yet another one of his favorite movies. "But for other people, the sick ones, it can take almost nothing to get them flying into a murderous rage. For instance, just cutting someone off in traffic. People have been shot for less."

He had a point. Unfortunately, there were a lot of people on that ledger of hers. It would take time to check them out one by one. And time was something we were running short of.

"Well, I plan to start with the ones who had the most motivation and work my way down from there. Maybe I'll get lucky and it will be one of the three I wrote down."

"Just because they're the obvious choices doesn't mean they're guilty, or innocent, for that matter."

I gave him one of Opal's looks. I'd been practicing. I must not have it down quite right yet, though, because all it got was a chuckle.

"Yeah, keep working on that."

I went to the cooler that we had stocked with ice and sodas and pulled one out for each of us. After handing him one, I asked, "Okay, so what's second of all?"

He looked confused. "What?"

"You said first of all that Sonya wasn't nice. I already knew that. But if there's a first of all, then there's a second of all, right?"

"Well, yes, at least in this case there is. I have a friend who transferred down to the Oak Hill Police Department. While you were napping, I made a call."

My heart sped up. "You didn't tell him you knew where Arc was, did you?"

He was much better at Opal's look than I was. I took that as a no.

"All I told him was that Archimedes Mineheart was a long-lost relative of my girlfriend and that she was worried that he might be being framed for the murder charge . . ."

Opie said a few more things, but by then, I was totally zoned out.

"Amie?" He waved his hand in front of my face. "Earth to Amie."

I snapped out of it, and my eyes focused on him again. He was giving me that lopsided smile. "It was the girlfriend thing, wasn't it?"

After swallowing the lump in my throat, I nodded. "Is that what I am now? Your girlfriend?" I held my breath. After all, it could have just been an embellishment told to get access to information from his friend.

Opie stood up and walked over to me. "I'd like you to be. But usually girlfriend status is kind of a two-way street. Both parties have to agree to it."

I thought about it. Did I agree? It surprised me to find that the answer was an immediate yes. With an exclamation point. How cool would it be to have your best friend as a boyfriend? And why on earth had it taken me all these years to realize that?

"I think I'd like that too. As long as we agree that even if the boyfriend slash girlfriend thing doesn't work out, we still keep the best friend status." I couldn't bear to lose him. If a few days almost killed me, what would the rest of my life do? Probably finish the job.

The next thing I knew, his lips were on mine.

And then my hair started floating.

"Ouch!" Opie stepped back from me. "I've heard that attraction can be electric, but—" Then he noticed my hair and took a couple more steps backward, stumbling into the table.

Crapsnackles. Not the reaction I wanted for our first kiss. I reached a hand out to him but stopped short of touching him. "Don't worry. I've got this."

After the incident at Opal's shop, she had made it a priority to teach me how to dispel magic harmlessly. It was far better than having to search for a sapling to grow, and far less exhausting too.

Closing my eyes, I imagined myself as a pool of cool spring water at the top of a mountain, water flowing into me from multiple sources. Then I concentrated on reversing the flow. Sending the water—or rather magic—out of me and back to its original source.

I'd caught this in time, before too much magic had accumulated, so it was a matter of seconds before I was back to normal. I wish I could say the same for poor Opie.

He was still backed up against the table with that same horrified look on his face.

"Is that going to happen every time we kiss?"

I took a deep breath. "I'm not sure. Maybe at first. For some reason, the magic seems to come whenever I get over-emotional." I gave him a sad smile. "That kiss was definitely the thing to get my emotions revving up." I was hoping he'd take that as a compliment.

Instead of looking happy, he just looked worried. "If a kiss does that . . ."

"Yeah, I've got some work to do." I swallowed. I wanted to ask if he was sure this was what he wanted after all, but I feared the truth to that answer would be no. I didn't think I could take that right now, and I didn't want my emotions to gear up again.

Finally, he reached out to me. His face was still crinkled with stress lines, but his eyes had a determined look to them.

Instead of a kiss, this time he just leaned his forehead down against mine. We stayed like that for a minute or two. It felt good, but not nearly as electrifying as the kiss had.

"I'll get there, I promise." It came out as a whisper.

"I know you will. And I'm not going anywhere this time." His voice was soft but firm. Opie meant what he said.

That gave me the calmness to do what I did next. Kiss him. Hard.

This time, my hair stayed in place. Right where it should be. It wasn't the same kind of kiss, though. I could tell that Opie couldn't really get into it. His eyes were open and staring at my hair.

My own personal early warning system.

I was the one who stepped back this time. "How's about we distract ourselves from all this for a bit with a little sleuthing?"

He nodded. "Sounds good. Where were you going when I got here?" Then he paused. "No, let me guess. The sexy school librarian?"

Opie always did know how my brain worked.

I glanced over at the clock. The day had gotten away from me. It was actually early evening. My stomach rumbled, reminding me that all I'd had to eat all day was a couple of donuts. It was demanding more.

Opie's stomach must have heard mine and decided to reply. It was enough to break the tension between us. Sometimes the Goddess worked in mysterious ways like that.

"Okay. How's about we grab some fast food first and then make our way to see the librarian?" he asked.

I nodded. "Excellent idea. But we have to be sure to get to her house before eight o'clock."

We were walking out the door when he paused. "What happens at eight?"

"Her internet show starts." I didn't think we really wanted to be there for that.

At least, I knew I didn't. Opie was a man. He might feel differently about it.

Chapter 12

By a quarter till seven, we were on the street in front of the sexy librarian's house. It was a small, well-maintained bungalow, and the landscaping was enough to make even a witch like me jealous.

I'd be asking myself how she could afford a cute little place like this in a good neighborhood, but I already knew the answer to that. She was selling herself on the side. Maybe it wasn't outright prostitution, but still, it was a far cry from a respectable way to earn a living.

"So, how do you plan on doing this?" Opie was looking at me.

I shrugged. He knew me well enough by now to know that I rarely had a plan for anything I did. I was a seat of your pants kind of girl.

"We're just here to chat, right?" I opened my car door and stepped out, but not soon enough to miss hearing Opie's groan.

I waited for him to come around the car, and then we walked up the short sidewalk and up the steps onto her porch. I was rather proud of our little second-story balcony at the farmhouse, but it wasn't nearly as ritzy as this place. Nothing so mundane as a porch swing or rocking chairs here.

Her seating consisted of some really cool, futuristic-looking hanging chairs with tables between each set of two. Hanging pots with flowers and vines surrounded them all. It was beautiful, but not nearly as cozy and warm as my little balcony. And that was what I'd keep telling myself too. All of our patio furniture probably didn't cost as much as one of those chairs.

Opie cleared his throat. Okay, yes, I'd been staring.

Straightening my back to give the impression of a little more height, I knocked on the door and waited. Within seconds, it swung open.

No safety worries here, apparently. Not if she was willing to open her front door wide to two strangers standing on her front porch. Especially as she was wearing nothing more than a thin silk robe.

Believe me when I say thin. It was obvious that she didn't have a stitch on under it. Tonight's show might just be starting a little early.

"Can I help you?" Her eyes glanced at me and then settled on Opie with an interest that I didn't take too kindly to.

That was my boyfriend she was ogling, dang it. Even if that would take some time to get used to.

A quick glance over at Opie showed the ogling went both ways. At least, it did before I elbowed him in the side.

I took a short step forward to get her attention. "We wanted to talk to you about Sonya Ignacio."

Her eyes widened, and the blood seemed to disappear from her cheeks. She even took a tiny step back before she said, "Who?"

Yeah, not buying it, lady. For someone who spent so much time on camera, she was an even worse actress than I was.

"Sonya Ignacio." I paused. "I believe the two of you had a small business arrangement?"

She swallowed and then looked at Opie as if for help. Finally, she opened the door even wider and stepped back. "You might as well come in."

Once the door was shut behind us, she led us over to the couch, and then flopped down in a recliner. Her head went into her hands, and her shoulders started shaking.

Was she crying? Was that a sign of guilt?

I glanced at Opie, but he seemed just as clueless to what her actions meant as I was.

"Ms. Miller? Are you okay?"

She took a deep breath and then sat up, defiance in her still watering eyes. "No, I'm not okay. I thought this nightmare had ended, but it hasn't, has it? You two are here to continue sucking me dry just like Sonya. What is it you want? My grandmother's china? That seemed to be next on Sonya's list."

"We don't want anything like that," Opie said quietly. "We just want to talk."

She sniffed and grabbed a tissue from the table beside her. "Then talk."

"Where were you the night Sonya was killed?"

Her gaze flew to me. For the record, the question seemed to totally take her by surprise. "What?" Then she looked at Opie. "But she was killed by her boyfriend, wasn't she? I heard they found her dead in his bedroom."

"That's where she was found, yes, but not where she was killed. Someone is trying to frame Archimedes for the murder."

"That's awful! I've met him a couple of times. I have to admit that I kind of liked him."

A gorgeous man like Arc? Somehow that didn't surprise me.

"So, could you answer my question, then?"

She tilted her head at me. "What question?"

"Where were you the night Sonya was killed?" If this was an act, it was a good one. Maybe I'd been wrong about her acting skills. Perhaps she just needed a little time to get into character first.

One hand flew to her chest. "You don't think I had anything to do with that?"

I was getting a little impatient. I'd asked twice, and she had yet to give an answer. Opie must have noticed my tension, because he decided to step in.

"We aren't saying anything like that," he said.

We weren't? Then why were we here?

"Right now, we're talking to all of Sonya's . . . business partners to see where they were that night and what they might have seen." He shrugged. "Oak Hill isn't that large of a city. Someone had to have seen something, right?"

She nodded slowly. "Maybe. But not me." Then why did she look so very guilty? "I was entertaining that night. Kind of a reward for my online followers."

"You had people here?" I asked. "How many, and can they verify that you were here all night?"

Her eyes narrowed as she turned to me. "Funny, but that doesn't sound like innocent questions to me. I think I'll deal with him, if you don't mind."

That tore it. I took a step forward, but Opie held me back. "That's fine, Ms. Miller, you can deal with me. Amie here will just stand quietly and listen. Is that okay?"

It took a minute, but she finally nodded. "I guess. And yes, I had people here. Two men, actually. Winners of a contest I held online. That's where you'll find the proof of my alibi—online. The timestamp of our video should be pretty conclusive."

"You were streaming live that night?" Opie seemed interested. A little too interested. "Do you do that often?"

She wiped her wet cheeks with another tissue and smiled at him. "Three times a week, but that one was special. As I said, it was the prize in a contest I held with my viewers."

I was starting to get a picture that my mind really didn't want to accept. In a word . . . eww.

"Well, that should be it, then. Except for one thing—do you know anything that might help us find who really killed Sonya? Anyone who might want her out of the way?"

"No, but to be honest, I'm quite sure I wasn't her only 'business partner,' as you put it. Any one of us had reason to want her out of the picture. She was bleeding us dry."

"If you think of anything, give me a call." Then he handed her one of his cards. I wanted to snatch it out of her hand, but I contained myself. Opie and I would have a long talk later about proper boyfriend behavior. Giving your phone number out to sexy, near-naked women wasn't on that list.

Once we were back in the car, Opie turned to me. "I shouldn't have given her my card, should I?"

Maybe there was hope for him yet.

***

We were heading back to the hotel when my cell phone went off. It wasn't a number that I recognized, so I started to swipe to cancel the call. Opie took the phone from my hand and answered it.

"Amethyst Ravenswind's phone."

I was leaning over in my seat, but there was nothing but silence on the other end. Grabbing the phone back, I said, "Who is this?"

"It's Arc. Was that your cop buddy who answered your phone? I'd hoped he'd gone back home by now."

"Nope. He's my new partner. You should be grateful instead of surly, you know. He's a dang good cop, and a good person to have on your side."

"Yeah, well, tell that to the rug burns all over my body."

Opie must have heard that part, because he was grinning. I really didn't think the two of them would ever be fast friends. But then, I'd been wrong before.

"You just calling to complain, or did you have some news for me?"

"Actually, I was calling to see where you were. I'm pretty sure I told you that Lily doesn't like it when people are late."

Late? To what?

"Huh?" That was my elegant response.

"The nightly dinner at Lily's. You know, so we can all regroup and discuss what we learned during the day? Remember?"

Nope. Not a single bit of it. "Sorry, but I don't recall being told that would be a nightly thing." I looked over at Opie. "I'm willing, but there will be an extra person coming. Is that okay with Lily?"

"Let me guess, your new partner?" He didn't sound happy.

I heard Lily in the background, and then she was on the phone. "Arc didn't tell you to come tonight, did he?"

"No, ma'am, he didn't." Then, feeling a little guilty for throwing him under the bus, I decided to add to that. "But things did get a little crazy for a while at the hotel. It most likely slipped his mind in all the excitement." There, that should make up in part for the rug burns.

"Hmm, well, if you say so. Are you close? We're having call in pizza tonight. Plenty for an extra mouth too." I could hear the smile in her voice. "We are actually quite looking forward to meeting your young man."

There was a short pause.

"Especially, of course, your father."

It might sound odd, but it took those words for me to get the big picture. I liked Arc, and finding out that he was my brother was a heck of a shock, but one I could deal with. I just hadn't actually put the rest of the puzzle together yet. Her words locked that last piece tightly into place.

Archimedes Mineheart Sr. was my father.

Where was a paper bag when you needed one?

Chapter 13

I didn't bother to tell Lily that Opie and I had already eaten. I mean, it was pizza. The two of us having already had drive-thru hamburgers and fries just meant that we'd eat more like normal people. Three or four slices each, tops. Normally, we could down a whole pizza just by ourselves. Extra-large, at that.

The street outside Lily's house was lined with cars. One of them I recognized instantly. Opal was here. Most likely, that meant Ruby was too. Kind of made sense. I'd been waiting to hear from her all day. Opal must have convinced her to wait and come with her. At least one of us had actually gotten the invitation.

Ruby gave me a hug first thing, then stood back and looked between me and Opie. "You two okay now?"

Opie blushed, but I just nodded. "For the most part, yeah. We still have a few things to work out, but I guess we're kind of a couple now."

"About dang time," Opal said. She was standing next to Merlin and Lily, looking into a large box.

Curious as to what could be holding their interest, I walked over. Box first, pizza later. That was a first for me.

Inside the box was a smaller white mother cat with three kittens. The baby cats were nursing, so they were contained and happy for the moment. I immediately started sneezing.

"Oh, I'm so sorry, dear," Lily said. "I totally forgot that you were allergic to cats. Just a moment." She nodded to Merlin, who reached down and touched each tiny body in turn.

Instantly, the tickle in my nose vanished. I had to know that spell. It was nothing short of a miracle.

He smiled up at me, still kneeling by the box. "I'll teach you the spell, but I warn you, it takes practice. But it's well worth it once you master it."

I'd say. "How long does it last?"

Merlin shrugged. "Couldn't say. I haven't seen it wear off an animal I've spelled yet."

"Ah, there you two are." Arc came in the back door from the deck. "I see you've met my familiar, Baxter." He frowned. "Gotta come up with a girl name equivalent now, don't I?"

I laughed. "You didn't know she was pregnant?"

The color rose on his cheeks. "Well, considering the fact that I thought she was a he, no. I didn't."

"She's not your familiar anymore, either, Arc," Senior said gently. "Now she's just a normal everyday cat with kittens."

"Having babies breaks the binding?" I was curious. I mean, it wasn't like that could be the answer to our little problem. Arc would not be getting pregnant anytime soon.

Senior laughed. "No. In fact, I was really curious as to whether or not the familiar spell would pass on to them." He shook his head. "Sadly, we'll never know. When you made Arc your familiar, it broke their binding."

Now all of us were staring at him.

"What? Do I have pizza stuck between my teeth or something?"

"Are you really saying that all it takes to break a familiar binding is to simply create a new one?" Opal got the question out first.

Senior nodded toward the box. "It would certainly appear so. Merlin said when she showed up at his house, the binding was no longer in place. If it had been, we could have traced it to find Arc."

"And when the witches' council showed up looking for her, they could have too." Merlin glanced at me. "As much as I hate to admit it, you making Arc your familiar really saved his bacon. If not for that, he'd be in a magic-blocked cell right now."

I swallowed, the hope that had sprung up with the seemingly easy solution taking a nosedive into my stomach. The binding spell between us must have been what changed Arc's signature. Not much, but enough to throw the council off our tails.

If we broke the binding now, they'd be on him in a matter of minutes. I was stuck with the magic for a bit longer. But it gave me a little hope. I really wanted to try that kissing thing with Opie again soon, and I wanted him to enjoy it too. Not be watching my hair the whole time.

"How old does a kitten have to be before they can become a familiar?" Baxter, or whatever her name was now, had three adorable babies. The fact that they would now be allergy-free was an added bonus. A big one.

"I'd wait until they were weaned. So, you're looking at a couple more weeks, anyway. That should give us time to put all this behind us." Senior obviously was a glass half full kind of guy.

Worked for me, but I might need to have some genetic testing done. With two optimistic parental units, how on earth did I end up . . . well, me?

"I do have one tiny question, though," I said looking over at Arc. "You got away from the trinity by changing into a Baxter lookalike, right?"

He nodded.

"Then why weren't you a white cat when I found you at the shelter?"

Senior ruffled his son's hair and grinned. "Probably because Arc here was smart enough to know that the council would be looking for a white cat."

Ah, that made sense.

***

The rest of the evening passed pleasantly enough. I filled in the others about what I'd found on Sonya's computer, and I found out that the others had been doing a little sleuthing on their own too.

Of course, we'd all ended up with nada for our first day out, but hey, at least it was a team effort. It was nice to know that it didn't all rest on little ol' me. I was still new to this.

The real shocker was when Opal had announced that she was closing the shop until we got this wrapped up. I couldn't remember the last time the shop had been closed for longer than a two-day stretch. Probably because it had never happened before.

Then I realized that with her position on the council's board, she was in this up to her neck. By knowing where Arc was and not reporting him, or even better, turning him over single-handedly, she was risking a lot. Quite possibly more than anyone else here. I mean, even if they found Arc and took him in, we could still prove his innocence and get him freed. But when one betrayed the council—well, let's just say they didn't take kindly to treason within the ranks.

We had to get this solved fast. I didn't want Opal paying the price for me bringing her into this. Or Ruby, either, for that matter. They were in danger of being in the council's bad graces because of their loyalty to me. And maybe to Mom.

Senior took the responsibility of checking out the hit-and-run businessman, and Merlin insisted on being the one to talk with the unfaithful wife. Both of them knew the people involved and thought that they could get more to the truth of the matter than I could.

At least, that was what they said. Personally, I believed it was more a matter that they didn't trust me to be all that diplomatic in my questioning. The fact that they were probably right about that kept me from questioning their opportunity to go first.

Besides, I had other avenues to pursue. Like that missing warded key that everyone else seemed to have forgotten about.

I wanted a talk with this Ryan Shea.

Chapter 14

After seeing me back to the hotel, Opie went back to Wind's Crossing. He had an early morning doctor's appointment for a follow-up on his leg wounds, but I really didn't think that was the reason he didn't stay the night.

He was scared. Truthfully, I was too. Now that I'd finally come to the realization that Opie was my soul mate, I was naturally curious to take it to the next level. But then there was the whole uncontrolled magic thing.

The best thing for my newfound budding love life would be for me to find the killer. Once that was done, I'd be free to break the binding and get rid of this cursed magic. Why had I ever thought having magic would be a good thing?

My alarm didn't wake me the next morning. Probably because it never got the chance to. I'd done my research and found that Ryan worked as a waiter in an upscale restaurant downtown. From what Arc had said, he really raked in the dough there. Much more money than I ever made with any of my endeavors. Maybe I'd been in the wrong profession all these years.

Then again, my disposition probably wouldn't be the kind to persuade patrons to leave me big tips. Or any tips at all.

Anyway, my plan was to go to the restaurant for lunch, a little treat for myself, and ask for a seat at one of Ryan's tables. If he was my waiter, then he couldn't very well not talk to me, right?

Since I had nothing planned until lunchtime, I'd decided to sleep in. Yeah, that didn't happen.

I answered the door, ready to blast whoever was standing on the other side. Unfortunately, it was Ruby. No blasting today. At least, not this morning. The day was still young.

"Hey, Ams." Then I noticed that she was holding two large bags.

I stepped back and let her in. "What's with the bags?"

She grinned at me. "I'm moving in. Opie doesn't want you here alone, and he says it's too early in your relationship for him to stay." She rolled her eyes. "Yeah, right. How long have we all been waiting for you to wake up and smell the aftershave?"

Had everyone known Opie's feelings but me? Dang, some investigator I was if I couldn't see something so close to me. I'd always known that Opie was a handsome guy. I wasn't blind. I'd always thought that the girls in our class at school were really missing the boat by not jumping on him. I had just never realized I was one of them.

As it was Ruby, I couldn't stay mad at her for long. Especially seeing as how she brought breakfast. Not just donuts, which was our usual quick eat morning meal, either. No, she brought piping hot biscuits and gravy over scrambled eggs with a side of hash browns. She had to have used a touch of magic to keep them this hot all the way from Wind's Crossing, but I wasn't going to complain. But that did bring up a question.

"How did you get here, anyway?" Ruby's only means of dependable transportation was her bicycle. No way would she have ridden this far on her bike. Especially with two large bags and a piping hot breakfast. And I hadn't recognized any of the cars outside, either.

"Have you heard of this little thing called Uber?"

I raised an eyebrow. "You called an Uber? Really?"

In the past, before I'd gotten my set of wheels with its very own motor, I'd often suggested calling them for a ride. Ruby had shot me down every single time.

She shrugged. "You gonna complain about it?"

I thought for a minute. Sure, I could bring up all those times I had sore calf muscles for a week or so after a long ride through the country to reach some destination we had in mind. But what good would that do?

"Nope." Part of that was because she was still in possession of the aromatic breakfast. Don't think I didn't know that Ruby knew that too. Confused yet? Just keep in mind that Ruby could be manipulative and devious when it came to getting her way.

She set the food down on the tiny table that was getting as much use as the room's beds, and we dug in with gusto. The first bite pretty much had me melting in my chair. I'd forgotten how good a full breakfast could be.

"So, what's on the agenda today?" At least she'd waited until we'd slated our hunger for the most part.

"I'm having lunch at one of the local eateries and questioning a waiter who works there." I filled her in on what little I knew about Ryan Shea.

"Wards can have keys? That's so cool." She looked thoughtful. "I don't know why I didn't think of that, actually. It's brilliant."

"Well, Earth witches are known for their protection spells. It's kind of their bag."

She nodded. "Agreed. But still . . ."

If I let her get too deep into her thought process, I'd lose her to a full day of magical experimentation. I'd seen it happen too many times over the years.

"For now, I think we just need to focus on the fact that wards can have keys, and not so much on the magical spell that allows them to work, okay?"

It took a minute for her eyes to focus on me. She looked very conflicted. Ruby loved her magic. I might like it, too, if I had any kind of control over it.

"You're right, of course." She didn't sound happy about it, though. As soon as this was over, or heck, if there was a brief interlude while it was still going on, Ruby would be testing out wards and keys. She might be able to read me like a book, but it went both ways.

I picked up the now empty plastic containers and threw them into the small trash can. It might be time to put out the housekeeping sign. The trash was almost overflowing. We hadn't wanted them coming in without warning because . . . well, there had been a fugitive staying there at first. Now that he was gone, we could update housekeeping to do their thing on a daily basis.

It was a little thing, but a nice feature for staying at a hotel. No bed making, dusting, or vacuuming required. Too bad I couldn't afford the luxury for very long. I'd paid a week in advance. When those days were done, I'd be working from the farmhouse and driving back and forth every day.

Gas was cheaper than a hotel. Even a cheap one like this.

We spent the morning catching up. I told her everything I knew about the case, and she told me about the goings on back at the shop. She was as surprised as I was about Opal closing up for an indefinite period of time.

"It isn't like she needs the money, you know."

That got my attention. She didn't? I'd assumed that Opal was just like the rest of us and living paycheck to paycheck.

"Grams was kind of loaded. When she passed, she left it all to our moms equally. By that time, they'd already paid off the mortgage on the house, so it was pretty much all just put into the bank for emergencies." She blew out a breath. "I really wish that Mom would see me not having a car as an emergency. It sure is to me."

I could understand that. I'd felt the same way myself just a few weeks ago. But then, I hadn't known about the large bank account just sitting there, either.

More than likely, the moms hadn't provided us with cars because as long as they kept us on bikes, they limited our ability to get into long-range trouble. I couldn't say it didn't work, either. It did. All too well. If we got into trouble, it was close enough to home that the moms knew about it fast. Usually before we'd even made it home.

I kind of liked being a few towns over from Wind's Crossing where no one really recognized me as a magic-less screw-up. It was a refreshing change of pace.

"I don't suppose you brought some of that truth serum spell with you?" I hated to ask, but it would make it much easier if we could be sure that whatever Ryan told us was the truth and nothing but the truth. Especially when it came to the whole losing the key thing.

She flushed and turned away. "I brought the ingredients, but I'm really hoping you won't make me use them."

I looked at her. Since when had Ruby ever not wanted to do a spell?

"Out with it."

"Mom really read me the riot act about using a truth spell on Arc. We got lucky that we actually had his permission first. Apparently, the council takes a very dim view of witches using spells like that on people without their consent. They call it magical manipulation, or something like that."

"But that guy at the retreat . . ."

Her face got even redder. "Yeah, let's hope Mom never finds out about that. Or the council. I guess I could get in real trouble over it."

"Mum's the word with me. You know that."

"Thanks."

I guess when we questioned Ryan, we'd just have to do things the old-fashioned way. Guts and female intuition.

Chapter 15

I had planned to get to the restaurant around noon, when I'd be sure that Ryan would be on duty. Ruby nixed that.

"If this place is popular, then waiting until the busy lunch rush isn't such a good idea."

My biscuits and gravy were still digesting when we stood in line at the doors of the eatery. I hated to admit it, but Ruby had been right. If there was a line at eleven, we might not have gotten in at all at noon. And if we had, it's a pretty safe bet that there would have been an hour or two's wait before eating. Not that my stomach would have minded the chance to deal with the hearty breakfast first.

As it was, we got the last table for the early lunch seating. Ruby looked especially proud of herself. She loved being right as much as I hated being wrong.

We got lucky that the last table happened to be in Ryan's area, or we might have had to wait after all. The hostess led us to the comfortable, plushy-cushioned booth and took away two of the four place settings. The menus were standing in a rack at the table. Kind of low-key for such a fancy place.

I'd barely opened the menu when the hostess was back.

"I'm so sorry," she said, returning the extra place settings to their original places. "I didn't realize you had others joining you."

Huh? I opened my mouth to tell her we didn't, when I saw Mom and Senior coming up behind her.

When they reached the table, Mom leaned down and gave me a peck on the cheek before taking the chair Senior held out for her. "So sorry we're late," Mom said. "Thanks for getting us a table."

"Sure, no problem." Then I waited until the hostess had gone back to her station. "What are you two doing here?"

Mom's face was glowing. "Isn't it obvious, dear? It's probably the same thing you're doing here." Then she turned to Ruby. "Hello, dear. My, but it's good to spend time with the two of you again."

I glanced around before leaning across the table. "I thought you guys were checking up on the hit-and-run guy."

Senior nodded. "We did. It isn't him."

Tilting my head, I waited. I was going to need more than just his say so before scratching the man off the suspect list.

Finally, he blew out a breath. "Look, Dylan has had a drinking problem for a while now. Hitting that woman . . . well, it woke him up. Then when Sonya tried to blackmail him, he just couldn't take the guilt any longer. It wasn't what Sonya wanted, but he went into rehab, and when he came out, he turned himself in. Turned down the opportunity for bail, too. I think he really wants to set things straight as much as he can."

"He was in jail at the time Sonya was killed?"

"Yes. I would have known that had he come to me for legal representation as he should have. But he didn't. I think he wants a long sentence out of this." He grunted. "As if him going to prison will change anything."

Mom patted the back of his hand. "It's his choice, dear. You're just going to have to deal with it." Then she reached over and grabbed a couple of menus, handing the extra one to her new husband. "And don't let the prices shock you two. Lunch is on Archie and me."

Surely it couldn't be that . . . holy cow! They wanted how much for a hamburger? I could buy stock in McDonald's for that price. Swallowing, I nodded. "That would be very nice."

The waiter who approached our table wasn't anything like I'd pictured him to be. I guess with him being a friend of Arc's, I'd expected another handsome man with a strong chin and a somewhat overbearing personality.

None of that applied. Ryan Shea wasn't ugly, but handsome wasn't a word that would describe him, either. He was . . . average. It was hard to tell while I was sitting down, but I was guessing him to be around five feet ten inches or so, and he weighed maybe two hundred pounds. He wasn't fat, but he wasn't exactly skinny, either. Again, everything about him was average. Right down to his dark brown hair and blue eyes.

"Are you all ready to order?"

Archimedes . . . Archie, I guess . . . did a double take. "Ryan? I can't believe I forgot you worked here."

I really had to practice my acting skills. Even I believed him for a second, and I knew better.

A brief emotion flashed over Ryan's face, but it was gone too quickly to put a certain name to it. Fear? Anxiety? Or maybe he'd just eaten a bad clam or something.

"Yup. I'm here until something better comes along, anyway." He hesitated and then glanced around at the full dining room. "I'd love to chat, but the manager likes the busy lunch hour to go smoothly."

"I understand completely," Archie said with a smile.

We asked for a few more minutes to choose our meals, and Ryan stepped away from the table. On a whim, I stood and told them I was going to use the lady's room. Something seemed off about Ryan, and I wanted a crack at figuring out what it was.

As I rounded the corner behind him, I saw him talk to the hostess and then head toward the door. I had to double step to catch up with him. He was really booking it.

"Ryan!"

At first it seemed like he was going to ignore my call, but finally, he turned to face me.

"Is something wrong? Why are you leaving?"

He hesitated, then pulled out his phone. "My girlfriend just texted me. She's having car trouble, and I need to go help her."

"Isn't that going to get you in trouble? That doesn't sound like a smooth lunch hour to me."

Ryan shrugged. "They can fire me if they want. In fact, it would probably be best if they did. I hate this place." He peered into my face. "Do I know you?"

The way he asked gave me a chill down my spine. Like he really didn't know if he should know me or not. How weird was that?

I shook my head. "No, but we have a friend in common." I hesitated and glanced around, trying out the whole acting thing. "I'm kind of helping Arc out right now. I was hoping I could talk to you for a minute."

His eyes widened, and I noticed his Adam's apple bobbed a few times before he said anything. "Is he okay? They haven't caught him yet, have they?"

"No. He's lying low right now, but he can't get out and about without risking being seen, so I'm doing the running for him."

"I see. What did you want to talk about?"

"First of all, you know Arc didn't do it, right? Kill Sonya?"

"Of course he didn't. Those two were tight. No way would he hurt her."

So why didn't his voice match his words?

"Well, we're trying to figure out how the killer got into his apartment to dump her body. Arc said you stayed with him for a while. Did you have a key?"

His face lost just a touch of color. "Are you accusing me of murder?"

"No, I just wanted to know if you still had the key. Arc said you may have lost it. If that's right, I wanted to know if you had any idea where you lost it."

He didn't look like he believed me. "I did lose it. But if I knew where I lost it, then it wouldn't be lost now, would it?" He waggled his phone at me. "Look, if that's all you wanted, I really need to be going."

And he turned and walked off down the street.

I watched him climb into a late model Chevy Camaro and drive off before turning to go back into the restaurant.

The manager caught me as I walked past the hostess station. "Is he coming back?"

Turning to him, I shrugged. "I don't think so. Not for a while, anyway. He said his girlfriend was having car trouble."

"Well, that's the last straw, as far as I'm concerned. He used to be a really good worker, but something changed when he got back from his little vacation. Now he just does the bare minimum, and the customers aren't liking it."

I remembered what Arc said about Ryan losing his brother and how that could change a guy. Maybe he'd been right.

After all, I had just found out about Arc, and if I lost him, I'd definitely be feeling it.

I liked him. And having a brother was kind of cool.

Losing him wasn't something I planned on doing anytime soon. Not to the witches' council, not to the cops, and not to whoever the heck was trying to put him behind bars for something he didn't do.

Arc was right. Losing a brother, even if you hadn't had him long, could really change a person.

***

The rest of the lunch had passed pleasantly. It was kind of nice spending time with Mom and . . . Dad. Man, was that ever going to take some getting used to. Funny how I could totally accept that Arc was my brother, even if it was a bit of a shock, but Senior being my father was really throwing me for a loop.

When we finished, Ruby and I headed back to the hotel for another look at Sonya's ledger to see if there were any possibilities that I had missed. Like Opie had said, some people kill for very small things. It wouldn't hurt to look at all of them, but going top to bottom in seriousness of secret just made sense.

Opie's car was parked two spaces down from my room, but he was nowhere in sight. That was kind of weird. Then he came strolling out of the room next to mine, grinning.

"I wrapped things up back home, so I decided to take a mini vacation while I finish out my medical leave. Oak Hill seemed like a good choice."

I'll bet it did. Probably exactly what he had in mind when he sent Ruby down here. I couldn't really complain about him getting a room of his own if both my beds were taken, now could I?

We all went in to check out Opie's room. It was just as nice as mine. I'd thought maybe mine was a one-shot deal, but no. Turns out if you could get past the exterior looks of this place, you had a quite pleasant place to stay.

His room only had a single bed . . . a king-sized one, no less. I filed that information for future reference, and we headed back to my room, with its better options for seating.

Ruby and I plopped down on my bed, and Opie settled on Ruby's.

"So, any news from your cop friend at the department?"

He grinned at me. "Actually, yes. I just treated him to lunch and pumped him for information. He really doesn't think Arc did it. According to him, there was no way Sonya was killed there, and no one but a crazy person would bring a dead body home with them." Then his grin faded. "The rest of his department don't seem so sure about that. They still want to talk with Arc pretty badly."

I could understand that. The problem was that if Arc talked to the police, even if they didn't hold him, the council would have the opportunity to nab him. And they would make the most of it too.

"That can't happen. Not until we find out who the killer is and can offer him up."

"Or her," Ruby said.

I nodded. There were plenty of women on Sonya's list, and women could be killers too.

"Are they looking at anybody else in particular?" I asked.

"As a matter of fact, yes. They also seem very interested in Stan Grayson, owner of Firestorm something. I guess it's a demolition company? Anyway, he was Sonya's boss."

Sounded about right. He'd said the cops weren't exactly leaving him alone about the case.

"Is there a reason they are looking at him?" Ruby asked.

I'd met the man. I was pretty sure of the reason, and I was right.

"My friend says that Grayson is a real slimeball, especially when it comes to women. He's had complaints of sexual harassment filed against him from former female employees." Opie paused for dramatic effect. "Sonya filed one herself just the day before she turned up as a dead body in Arc's bed."

Sounded fishy to me too. Had he killed her out of anger? Because she'd rejected him, or because she'd turned him in for inappropriate boss behavior? It was as plausible as any other theory we had going.

But there was still a major problem. How had he gotten past the Mineheart Fireworks Ward?

Had he found the missing ward key? Was there some connection between him and Ryan Shea?

Then it hit me. Of course there was. Sonya. What if Ryan had lost the key while visiting Sonya at work?

My brain was busy traveling down that road, when Opie handed me a thumb drive. I just looked at it for a minute.

"What's this for?"

"You need to copy all the files on Sonya's computer that you think might hold information. Then I'm taking it in to my friend. I've told him it's coming, so this is going to happen."

That had been the plan all along, anyway. Copying the files took a while, but in less than an hour, Opie was on his way to drop off the computer with his friend. I didn't know what story he would give the man, and I really didn't care. I trusted Opie.

"What's next?" Ruby asked from directly behind me.

I jumped. "Are you using Arc's quiet carpet spell? That's not fair, you know."

She laughed. "No, but it's fun. I changed it up a little. My version is the quiet shoes spell." She lifted a foot. "No one will ever hear me coming again."

I raised an eyebrow and looked pointedly at my own sneakers. She took the hint. It was a quick spell, and she was prepared with the ingredients she needed. I'd have to remember to have her do my hiking boots when we got home. Those things were noisy as heck.

Walking around the room afterward, I marveled at my soundless passage. This, I could get used to. A very handy spell, indeed.

"Okay, so now you have quiet shoes too. So, I repeat . . . what's next?"

She seemed excited. Ruby was really getting into the investigation part of things. She'd kind of missed out when I'd had my first case trying to clear her mom. Besides, that one had hit a little too close for comfort for her. Not something she could enjoy.

I'd be glad when the cases I worked on didn't involve family members. Maybe then I could enjoy them too. For now, I'd settle for just getting to the bottom of them.

"I was thinking maybe it might not hurt to revisit Stan Grayson."

We grabbed our bags and were ready to head out, when the knock came. I glanced out the window before opening the door, and my heart nearly froze in my chest.

It was Patricia Bluespring. The witches' council was at my door.

Chapter 16

The fact that she was alone gave me hope that it wasn't anything serious. If she'd been there to arrest me, or whatever the equivalent to that was for the council, she'd have two more witches with her. A full trinity.

I took a deep breath before I opened the door. I tried out a smile, but I didn't think it really came off the way I had intended.

"Hello, Ms. Bluespring."

"Amethyst. I'm here on official council business. May I come in?"

I had to think about it for a minute. It wasn't like she was a vampire or something. If she truly wanted in, she would be in already. But if she was waiting for an invitation?

"No. I don't think so. Unless you have a search warrant on you." I paused. "Does the council use search warrants?"

She didn't look happy. "No, we do not. But fine, we can do what's necessary right here, then."

"And what would that be?"

"I'm here to put a sight and sound traveling spell on you."

Not if I had anything to say about that. The spell she was talking about would allow the council to watch me and hear any conversations I might have from wherever they happened to be. I couldn't imagine that even the council would go to such extremes on an innocent witch, and they had nothing on me. If they did, there'd be two more witches at my door.

I gave her a look. "Doesn't that type of spell fall under the magical manipulation that is frowned upon by the council?" Thank you, Ruby, for that little tidbit.

She didn't look happy that I knew about that. She'd probably thought me to be ignorant when it came to council rules and regulations. Which I had been, right up until this morning.

"An innocent witch with nothing to hide would be more than willing."

Is that so? Personally, I couldn't imagine any sane person being willing to give up their right to privacy.

"Why me? Is this because my magical signature is too close to Archimedes Junior's? I don't think that breaks any council sanctions. It's not like it's something I can control."

Her face would have given lemons a lesson on how to be sour. "That little mystery has been solved. Archimedes Mineheart Sr. has claimed you as his child. It's still odd that your signature is as close to Junior's as it is, but at least now we know the why behind it."

She leaned toward me, her eyes narrowing. "I know you are hiding him. It would be better if you came clean and let the council do its job."

"I'm not hiding him. In fact, I have positively no idea where he is right now, or what he is doing." Literally the truth. He could be at Lily's or out taking a feline stroll around the block for some air for all I knew. "But answer me this: why do you hate the Minehearts so much? Even the police don't think Arc killed Sonya. Why do you have your heart set on him being the killer?"

"You're wrong about the police. They are looking for him just as hard as we are. And as for your question, I have a personal relationship with the Minehearts, so believe me when I say that the entire family is made up of nothing more than thieves and liars."

That was a little strong. I heard Ruby's gasp from over my shoulder. It drew Bluespring's attention to her.

"Oh, Ruby, I'm so disappointed to see you involved in all this. You had such potential."

And apparently, I had none, even before all this started. Yeah, I knew what the council thought of me. A waste of a good bloodline. Well, wouldn't they be surprised to find out I had magic now? Even if it was just temporary. And technically Arc's magic, now that I really thought about it. Probably wouldn't impress them much at all.

"I'm afraid I will need more than your say so on their character, Ms. Bluespring. They seem perfectly nice to me."

Her lips drew up, and I more than halfway expected her to spit at my feet. "Well, you're family now, aren't you?" She hesitated, her eyes beaming with hatred. "But if it's proof you need, ask Senior to show you my grandfather's pocket watch sometime. It's quite the rarity. Probably why he never returned it to me as he promised he would."

Didn't sound like the man I was getting to know. Or the type of man that my mom would marry. It was time to end this.

"I'll make you a deal, Ms. Bluespring. I'll agree to your sight and sound traveling spell . . ." Her eyes widened, and a smile started creeping over her lips. "If you'll agree to let me put one on you."

The smile shut down, replaced with a frown.

"After all, an innocent witch would have no reason not to agree to one, right?"

She growled, and her eyes flashed for just a second. That glowing green color of an animal caught in headlights at night. It was creepy as heck. Patricia Bluespring was no ordinary witch. She was something . . . else.

It took every ounce of willpower I had to stand my ground after seeing that flash, but I did. I was a Ravenswind, dang it.

She stood there for a full minute in silence before turning and walking back to her car without another word. What more was there left to say?

There was no question in my mind that Patricia Bluespring hated the Minehearts with a passion. The only question was: did she hate them enough to kill Sonya and frame Arc?

Right now, I'd have to say yes.

And I really wanted to know what the hell she was.

***

After the run-in with Patty Bluespring, I just didn't have it in me to face the leech in human clothing that was Stan Grayson. So, we ran to the nearest office supply store and picked up the cheapest printer they had. I wanted to have a hard copy of the file at hand. Something more mobile than the laptop that we could mark out names as we eliminated them as suspects.

We were getting good at marking names off. What we needed to be doing was circling one in red with a big bullseye around it. But every name that came off the list was one closer to that bullseye. I just had to keep that in mind.

As we printed off the names, we did what we could to research each person online. After an entire afternoon, we were still no closer than we had been before we started. But we had the beginnings of a plan. We'd numbered the remaining suspects from highest to lowest probability. Stan Grayson was at the top, followed by Patricia Bluespring, who was in turn followed by the mother with the illegitimate son, followed by a host of other blackmail victims.

We'd move down the list, visiting and investigating each one until we could reliably mark them off the list for good. Or, even better, circle them in that bright red bullseye.

Around six thirty, we headed for Lily's. No way was I going to be late again. She'd excused me last night. I didn't think I'd get the same favor the second time around.

Ruby and I were the first to arrive. I was glad, because that gave me time to ask Arc a few things.

"Is there any way for someone to know your ward key when they see it?" I would definitely be looking for it when I went back to Firestorm, but it would help a lot if I knew, you know, what it looked like.

Arc nodded. "Oh yeah. It's bright green, and if you clap, it glows so you can find it. Then if you don't pick it up in thirty seconds from the clap, it whistles."

Ruby laughed. "You have a whistling ward key?"

He looked pleased with himself. "No. I have a whistling ward key that glows. It makes it kind of hard to stay lost."

I thought for a minute. "Could we do a find spell on your magical signature?"

Arc grimaced. "I tried that. It didn't work. It kept leading me around in circles."

"That's odd," Ruby said. "Find spells are usually pretty accurate."

He shrugged. "But I'm trying to find my signature, and I've . . . well, I like my magic."

And obviously, he'd spread it around a lot too. Still, at least I could identify the key now. That was something.

The others started filing in, and Opal arrived with Yorkie Doodle in tow.

"Before you ask, I called to check with Lily to see if I could bring him. And I called the lodge where you're staying, and they allow small dogs, so you're okay there too."

Ruby picked him up for a snuggle. "I thought you wanted him to stay out of the way at the farmhouse."

"I did, at first. But now I'm going away for a couple of days, so you'll just have to make arrangements to not leave him alone too much."

"Where are you going?" I asked. It wasn't like the perfect time to take a vacation. But then again, the only thing she really had riding on this was her seat on the council. Although, I had to admit, I would have thought the whole treason thing would have her more concerned. But bottom line, she could leave if she wanted to.

She hesitated. "There's something I want to check out in Indianapolis. A clue. And no, I'm not telling you what it is. You do your thing, and I'll do mine."

"My caseload is pretty light at the moment," Merlin said, coming up behind Opal. "I can go with you, if you like."

All he got for his offer was one of Opal's signature stares—with extra ice. "Thank you, but that won't be necessary. I already have my traveling partner."

Mom stepped up. "Who would that be?"

Opal just looked at her. "You have your secrets, and I have mine. I'm keeping this one."

It was good that Opal wasn't going alone, especially if her trip had anything to do with the case. I'd still feel a whole lot better if I knew that whatever, or whoever, she was investigating wouldn't put her in danger.

And yes, I wanted to know who her traveling companion was too. I was hoping it was someone competent. Knowing Opal, they would be. She didn't suffer fools lightly.

"All right, everyone. Dinner is on the table. I hope you all like meatloaf. If not, there's ham and beans with cornbread too."

Lily obviously believed in being prepared. I respected that. Especially as meatloaf wasn't one of my favorite foods. I'd eat it if I had to just so I wouldn't be rude, but I was grateful that she'd prepared an alternative.

As always, the talk over dinner wasn't allowed to stray into what we all really wanted to talk about. The case. But that was okay. I was starting to have a healthy respect for Lily and her rules. They had seemed kind of a time waster before, but it was nice to have a small half-hour window each day where we at least pretended that everything was normal in our lives.

Afterward, we met back in the living room. The others took seats on the furniture, but me and Arc sat on the floor next to the kittens' box. They were active tonight, and I had yet to pick out which one would be mine.

It would be a hard choice. All three were adorable. One was a pure white except for a small bit of black at the tip of her tail. Another one was mostly black, with a little white mustache and eyebrows. And the last was a striking calico with a yin-yang face divided in color between black and orange.

Each one seemed to have their own personality too. Having never been able to be around kittens before due to my allergies, they fascinated me. Too bad a witch couldn't have three familiars. Then I wouldn't have to choose.

Merlin started off the case talk. "Okay, so I had a long talk with Karen Moore today about being on Sonya's list. She admitted to the blackmail but insisted that what Sonya had asked of her wasn't anything worth killing for. A simple favor that she would have done anyway if she'd asked her nicely, according to Karen."

"What was the favor?" Arc asked, scooping up the little white ball of fur for a quick cuddle.

I was content to just watch them. For now, anyway. I was still getting the hang of this being around cats thing. It was a good thing Yorkie Doodle was behaving himself. He'd shown some initial curiosity but had taken the momma cat's no as the final answer on the subject.

Good dog.

"According to Karen, all Sonya wanted was an invitation to a party that a friend of Karen's husband was throwing. One that had a lot of celebrity attendees. She got the distinct impression that Sonya was on the prowl for a rich and influential husband."

"But what was to stop Sonya from coming back later for more? Or letting her secret out, anyway?" I mean, it was a pretty big secret that her youngest child didn't have the father her husband thought she did.

Merlin shrugged that off. "Truthfully, I don't think Karen thought it as much of a threat as we all think it was. Glen's been known to see a few ladies behind her back too. She might just view it as getting a little vengeance on him. I don't think there is much love left in that marriage at this point."

Another name crossed off the list. That left us with two primes. Stan Grayson and Patricia Bluespring.

I was up next and told them about Bluespring's visit to our hotel.

"She really, really doesn't like you all, you know. And she's . . . not a normal witch, is she?" I was looking at Senior when I said it. Of all of us, he would know her the best. After all, he'd been married to her, even if the marriage hadn't lasted all that long.

He looked away and wouldn't meet my eyes. "Nothing about Patty is normal. She's a one of a kind for sure."

"What happened between the two of you that caused her to hate you so much?" Mom asked.

I held my breath and waited. Would he confess?

No. He just shook his head. "I have no idea. We parted amicably enough. She was the one to leave me, though it was a mutual agreement. There didn't seem to be any hard feelings at the time. Just something that didn't work out. I had hoped we could stay friends. That changed about a week later. I have no idea why."

"I think I do," I said quietly. Every eye in the room focused on me. "I asked her today why she hated you all so much. I kind of think it stems from you not returning her grandfather's pocket watch. I think it meant a lot to her."

He stared at me like I'd grown a second head. "But of course I returned it! I took it to her new place the very next . . ." his voice trailed off, and he started cursing. "I knew I shouldn't have given it to her roommate. There was just something about her that didn't feel right. At the very least, I should have followed up to be sure she got it."

Merlin's face was a little whiter than it had been. "That's bad, Archie. That watch was an heirloom with a lot of built-up family power behind it. Even in the hands of non-witches . . ."

Senior groaned. "I know. But the roommate wasn't a witch. All she would have seen was the money it would bring. I'll bet she sold it. And that was a couple of decades ago. How on earth do you trace something like that now?"

He put his head in his hands. "It's no wonder she hates me so much. She'll never believe me if I tell her now."

I glanced over at Opal. She was used to finding things for people. Her specialty was in finding one of a kind items. Precisely like the pocket watch at the center of Patricia's hatred. She gave me a small nod. She'd find it.

That didn't stop Patty from being a suspect. Her hatred was still firmly in place, even if it was unfounded.

Chapter 17

In the hotel room by the television was a sign-up offering complimentary DVD players upon request at the office. Opie hit the Redbox on the way home, even though I was a little leery of letting him choose the night's entertainment. I was really hoping the rental unit would be out of Ghostbusters.

When he came in with an actual comedy, I breathed a major sigh of relief. Finally, something worth watching. He'd even stopped by the store for two big plastic bowls and some microwave popcorn.

The movie was good, and the company was even better. I enjoyed having a small period of time to just relax and pretend things were normal. Kind of like Lily's dinner rules, but at my new home away from home.

I must have been more tired than I'd thought, because I dozed off sometime before the end of the movie. The sound of breaking glass and Ruby screaming woke me in a hurry.

Someone had thrown some kind of firebomb through the room's window, and it had broken against the foot of my bed and ignited the bedclothes. If I'd been in the room by myself, that probably would have been the end of Amethyst Ravenswind. But I wasn't alone.

Opie threw the flaming covers off the bed before the flames could make it through to me. I got a little scorched, but nothing like the burns I'd have gotten had the fire burned through the thick cover.

Ruby stepped in then and grasped my hand. "Sorry," she said, then I felt the magic flowing from me to her through our clasped hands.

Our hair started floating as Ruby quickly chanted, raising our arms together in a single fluid motion. When she brought them down, the fire snuffed out like someone blowing out a birthday candle.

Once he saw we were okay and the fire was out, Opie was running for the door. He didn't get far.

"Girls, come quick!"

The first thing I saw after stepping through the room's threshold was my precious baby engulfed in flames. Ruby and I did the magic thing again, but it didn't work quite as well as it had on the room. Probably because her magic had already been drained from the first spell.

Opie ran back into the room and came out with the fire extinguisher to polish it off. Far too late to save my wonderful freedom-giving car, but fast enough to stop any kind of explosion should the flames have reached the gas tank.

By now, people were gathering. I leaned against the side of the hotel as the manager rushed toward us.

"What the hell happened here?"

"I think someone just tried to kill my friends," Opie said. "Almost got all of us."

"And almost burnt down my bread and butter in the process." The manager, probably the owner, too, from the amount of worry on his face, stepped past us and into the room. When he came out, he looked a little relieved. "You guys must have acted very quickly. I appreciate that."

He paused, and I knew what was coming next. We were about to get our walking papers.

"I'm sorry, but I have to think about the safety of my other guests, and of the hotel itself. As greedy as that sounds, it's true." To give him credit, he didn't look happy about it. "You three need to leave. I'll refund the money for the rest of your stay."

I swallowed, then shook my head. "Keep the money I gave you. If it weren't for me, you wouldn't have this damage to fix. Hopefully it will help you cover the deductible on your insurance."

He nodded. "Thanks. I was kind of wondering how I would come up with that." Then he turned to my car. What was left of it. "Ouch."

Yeah, I had to agree with him there. Ouch, indeed.

"Come on, Amie," Opie said, reaching down a hand to help me up. Funny, but I didn't remember sitting down.

I stood with his help, and we went in to pack up our stuff. Luckily, nothing was damaged beyond the bed's footboard, the bedcovers, and the carpet by the bed. Well, besides the big gaping hole the bottle had made in the front window.

What was it with people and Molotov Cocktails, anyway? I was attracting the wrong kind of bad guy in my life. They really needed to switch things up.

Then I thought of Ruby's fast-acting spell. Maybe that wasn't what I wanted after all. She wouldn't have had that spell ready so fast if she hadn't already had experience with it.

"Are we going back to the farmhouse?" Ruby asked, placing her bags by the door. "Or do we try another hotel? Surely the town has more than one, right?"

I was having trouble thinking clearly. Was it the magic that had flowed from me to Ruby doing that? Were these the aftereffects of spellcasting? If so, then it was just one more reason to get rid of the blasted magic and go back to being my little ol' self again.

Ruby and Opal could have it.

"No to both those choices," Opie said, coming into our room carrying his bags. "This is a time for family to stick close together. There's safety in numbers." He eyed Ruby and me. "Especially with the kind of power you guys have."

Then he smiled and shook his head. "I sure am glad you all are the good guys. I'd hate to have to come up against you."

Never gonna happen.

"Besides, I have a place for us already in Oak Hill." Wow, that was fast. "I just got off the phone with Sapphire. We're expected at Senior's house in less than a half hour. Your mom was rather insistent."

Oh joy, nothing like living under your newly discovered father's roof to get to know him. But even I had to admit it offered perks. Especially as I no longer had a car to make the commute back and forth from the farmhouse.

Sure, I had insurance, but I was pretty sure getting new wheels wouldn't be an overnight thing.

With one last, sad look back at our now not so pretty room, I picked up my bags and followed the others out to Opie's car.

By the time we had the bags stowed in his trunk, the police arrived. How on earth had I forgotten that part of the process? I must be in more shock than I'd realized.

Needless to say, we didn't make it to Mom's in the promised time frame.

***

Senior's house was everything I'd expected it to be and more. This wasn't just the home of a prominent small-town attorney. This was the home of old money.

Well, I say home. Mansion is more like it.

Mom and Senior met us at the door. It was after midnight when we made it. Answering the police's questions repeatedly had taken a lot of time. And they hadn't been happy at all with our answers.

I was formally warned to stay off the murder investigation. According to them, that was a job for them, not me. My tongue was sore from biting it so hard. That and Opie's quick elbow was all that kept me from telling them it was me who came up with Sonya's computer. Their biggest break in the case to date.

What I was doing wasn't breaking any laws. And warning or no, I planned to keep right on doing it. After all, if the killer had tried to add me to the victim list, he had to know I was getting close.

Surely that narrowed things down? Tomorrow, when I had a clear head, I was really hoping my thoughts would all come together with a brilliant revelation. Until then, my brain seemed to be declaring a holiday.

Mom and Senior both had to give us all hugs, and then they led us inside, past the immaculate porch—and here I'd thought the sexy librarian's porch was nice. Senior's put hers to shame. No, there weren't any futuristic hanging chairs, but it was incredibly stylish in an old-fashioned way. My kind of porch.

Part of me wanted to cuddle up on one of his cushioned porch swings and pass the night swinging my cares away. If only it were that easy.

"I'm so glad none of you were hurt," Mom said, clicking her tongue. Her face had a far more serious expression than she normally allowed on it. "The sooner we get this figured out, the better. If that person hurts any of you . . ."

Okay, so Mom could be a bit scary. I'd seen that side of her only once before, back in my grade school days when we were dealing with a couple of witch-hating kids and their families. Normally, Mom was a very easy-going person. Not so when someone threatened a loved one.

If we'd been hurt or, Goddess forbid, killed, I know that Mom would have hunted them down to the very ends of the earth. And I wouldn't give you a plug nickel for their chances when she'd found them, either. I had a feeling Mom wouldn't stop with slamming them up against a wall.

Then again, I wouldn't have either, if Opal hadn't stopped me. Mom and I take the protection of our family very seriously.

"I know it's late tonight, so why don't we all try to get some rest and regroup in the morning? We can figure out tomorrow where to go from here." Senior's voice was kind and soothing. He made it sound like the best idea in the world.

We followed them up the stairs. A massive staircase with a curved oak railing and banisters led to the second floor of the house.

"Archie and I have rooms on the bottom floor," Mom said. "We pretty much live down there. I'm afraid it might be a bit dusty up here."

"We can live with a little dust, Ms. Ravenswind," Opie said, smiling at her. "Or is that Mrs. Mineheart now?"

Good point. How had I not thought about that? Right now, sure, I could blame my befuddled brain, but where had the thought been back when I'd been thinking straight?

She shook her head. "I kept my name the same, dear. But please, after all these years, I really do think you should just call me Sapphire." She looked over at me. "Or Mom, for that matter."

I blushed and turned away, taking the opportunity to look around. Not that I was avoiding her look or anything. But it occurred to me that maybe Opal wasn't the only one who wanted grandchildren in the near future.

The upstairs was every bit as grand as the rest of the house. At the top of the steps, there was a balcony of sorts that overlooked the big front room below. I could almost imagine the balls being held there. People dancing in fancy gowns below, and older, more respectable people watching from above. This place had a history; I was sure of it.

She led us to two doors side by side down a long hallway. Opening the first door, she motioned for Opie to go in. "You can sleep in here, Opie dear. There is a connecting door into the next room where I'll put the girls."

I glanced over his shoulder as he walked in and nodded. Yup, same as I'd expected. Beautiful, but not overbearing. It impressed me that anyone could take a mansion and actually make a comfortable home of it.

Ruby and I got the room next door. It held two twin beds, both with four posters and an amazing canopy topping them. A little girl's dream bed.

"There are plenty of rooms in this old place," Mom said, looking around to make sure we had everything we needed. "But I thought, at least for tonight, you three would want to be close together."

She was right.

I just hoped whoever had thrown those firebombs wouldn't realize where we had moved to. The last thing I wanted was to bring the trouble here.

Senior must have seen my worried expression. "Don't you worry about the safety here." He gave me a kind smile. "I've tweaked and expanded the wards just a bit since this all started. Trust me when I say that no one will get to the house without our knowing it."

I just nodded. I believed him. After all, that was Earth's special power. Protection.

I could sure use some of that now.

Chapter 18

It had been nice of Mom to give Ruby and I a single room. It felt a little like old times back at the farmhouse. We'd shared a room all the way through high school. Like here, there had been plenty of room for the two of us to have separate bedrooms, but neither of us had wanted that. We'd spent many a night staying up well into the wee hours of the morning talking.

Not tonight, though. I envied Ruby her ability to sleep no matter what. If only I'd inherited that little gene too. Maybe it was tied to the magical one.

When the sounds of her soft snoring wafted over to me, I realized I had two choices. I could go and invade Opie's personal space and crawl into bed with him, or I could find something to entertain myself until my brain felt capable of relaxing enough for sleep.

As Opie had made it clear that until I got my magic under control, he wasn't willing to risk any type of major affection sharing, that left me with finding something to do.

That's when it hit me that of all the online accounts and passwords we had of Sonya's, we'd only ever really looked at the ledger one. Who knew what a gander at the others might reveal?

I took the computer into the bathroom to boot it up so that its rather loud startup signal wouldn't disturb

Ruby. Once it was up and running, I propped myself up in bed and situated the computer on my lap. A glance at the other bed showed that Ruby hadn't even moved. Good.

Yorkie Doodle raised his head to look at me, but it lowered pretty quickly as he snuggled back into Ruby's side. Funny, but it made me miss Destiny. I'd only had a cat for a few days, but I'd liked it. The kittens couldn't get weaned soon enough to suit me.

Pulling up the passwords file, I went through the names of the online accounts. I ended up back in the online journal. That sounded like a good place to start. And there were plenty of other files there besides the ledger. Files I hadn't even looked at yet.

Once logged in, I saw that there were years' worth of Sonya's life experiences on there. Where to start? On the hunch that whatever had been the root cause of her death probably happened fairly recently, I started three months ago.

A couple of weeks in, I hit pay dirt. There had been mention of Ryan finding his long-lost brother before, but not anything I hadn't already known. This entry, however, was new.

I'm not sure how to tell Ryan my news. He has a right to know. He needs to know. But telling him will be admitting that I took the time to check out his brother. Ryan isn't going to like that.

But before Ryan goes down to Indianapolis to meet the man, he needs to know that his brother is a no-good scumbag. I don't want Ry-Ry getting hurt.

I had to take a minute to absorb a couple of things here. One was that his brother was in Indianapolis, which just so happened to be where Opal's little trip was taking her. I didn't know how she found out before I did, but then, Opal always had her ways around getting critical information before the rest of the world.

If she were willing to use her powers for evil when it came to the stock market, we'd all be filthy stinking rich. But no, she had her morals.

A glance at the clock showed that it was far too late to make a call. Yeah, right. If Opal hadn't wanted to be woken up in the middle of the night, she would have told me the reason for her trip before she left.

Grabbing my phone, I went back into the bathroom and shut the door. Opal answered on the third ring.

"This better be good."

I could play this one of two ways. I could go on the offensive and demand to know what she knew about Ryan's brother, or I could play the family card and pretend I was just calling to let her know what had happened tonight. No contest, really.

"Has Mom called you yet?"

There was a few seconds of silence. "No. What's happened?"

I took a few minutes to tell her about the night's activity. I heard her relaying the story to someone, and then she was back on the phone.

"Whatever you're doing, you must be getting close. Tell Ruby to do the personal protection spell on all of you. She can raid the supplies at the shop. Some of the ingredients are kind of hard to come by, and she will need plenty on hand."

"Got it." I hesitated, but curiosity got the better of me. "Who is that with you?"

"None of your damn business, that's who."

Yeah, that's pretty much what I'd expected her to say. Opal loved her secrets.

"Okay, I'll give you that one, but I really want an answer to this one. I need to know what you know about Ryan Shea's brother."

A grunt came over the phone. "Ah, you've found something, then, haven't you? No matter. His name was Roger Hendrickson, and he was bad news. In debt up to his eyeballs to all the wrong people. He'd even done some time in prison for drug trafficking. The man was no good."

"Okay, so why the trip to Indianapolis?"

She hesitated. "I'm not sure I want to say quite yet. I know you, and you're in enough danger as it is."

Another quiet conversation with whoever her new roommate was. As much as I perked my ears to try to make out the voice, I just couldn't quite get a grasp on its owner. It sounded familiar, though, so definitely someone I knew. But who?

"Okay, look. Maybe you should know this much. Roger Hendrickson didn't just die. He was murdered. And the cops don't have a clue who did it, either. I'm wondering how it all ties in, that's all. Roger's head was bashed in, same as Sonya's. Could be the same killer."

"And there's only one connection that I know of," I said quietly. Ryan Shea.

"Yeah. Stay clear of him until I learn more. We checked into a hotel just north of Indianapolis for the night. We'll spend tomorrow digging up what we can and then head back. If we don't make it back before Lily's dinner, I'll call it in."

Sounded fair enough. "Will you be bringing your guest?"

She laughed. "In your dreams, girl." And she hung up.

I said a little prayer to the God and Goddess to protect them, and then quickly expanded it to protection for all of us.

I had a bad feeling we would need it before all of this was said and done.

No way was I going to make it to go to sleep now.

There was someone else I really needed to talk to, and this one I wanted to do face to face. The trouble was that I didn't have a set of wheels anymore. Not even my bicycle.

I chewed my lip, thinking about my alternatives. A quick search on the internet told me that Lily's house was about five miles away. Too far away for a post-midnight walk in a town I wasn't familiar with. Especially considering the fact that there had been one attempt on my life already tonight.

There was always Uber, but I didn't like that idea one bit, either. That left Opie.

I crept into his room and stood by his bed, looking down at his sleeping form. At the sight of him, something in me relaxed. I just wanted to hold him. Just for a minute.

Crawling under the covers, I snuggled into his back and rested my arm gently around him. He sighed in his sleep and settled in even closer.

I closed my eyes for just a split second to revel in the closeness.

***

The next thing I knew, it was morning. Real morning, with the sun streaming in through the windows and everything.

I opened my eyes straight into Opie's gaze. Okay, that was a bit of a shock. It took me a minute to get my bearings. This was so much worse than the whole, where am I thing that normally came with waking in a strange bed.

"Why are you in my bed?" His voice sounded oddly strangled.

"Don't worry. I didn't take advantage of you if that's what you're worried about."

He took a deep breath. "Nope, pretty sure I would have remembered that. What I don't remember is you being in my bed."

I smiled at him. "I came in to ask you for a ride, and then . . . well, I just wanted a quick snuggle, you know?"

Opie sucked in a breath. "A ride?" Okay, now his voice was really strangled.

Frowning at him, I nodded. "I need to talk to Arc, but I don't have a car anymore, remember?"

He nodded, his face clearing and his breath going back to normal. He rolled over onto his back and closed his eyes. "And you fell asleep."

"Guilty as charged."

I was about to suggest we make the most of the current situation when, of course, Ruby walked in. She never was much of a one for personal boundaries. And yes, I saw the irony in me being the one saying that.

"I wondered where you'd gotten to." She sat on the side of the bed, grinning at us. "So, what's ya doing?"

"Nothing, with an audience," I said, throwing the covers off and setting my feet on the floor. "Besides, we have things to do. I need a ride over to Lily's. We need to have a talk with Arc."

I briefly caught them up to date, and then we each went our separate ways to get dressed and ready to go.

Showers were definitely in order. Laundry would be in order soon, too. The smell of smoke still clung to our skin and the clothes we had worn the night before.

Probably something we should have taken care of then, but it hadn't crossed our minds.

I went first for the shower in our shared bathroom, as I'm generally a three-minute lather and rinse kind of girl, and Ruby likes to dawdle. I didn't want to end my shower time with a quick burst of ice-cold water because Ruby had hogged all the hot. Happened all the time back at the farmhouse before I'd become self-employed. It was easier to share shower schedules now that I set my own work time.

Within a half hour, we were all dressed and headed down to Opie's car. We didn't quite make it.

Mom met us at the bottom of the stairs.

"I heard you all moving around up there, so I started breakfast. Wherever it is you all are off to can wait until after you've eaten."

Who could argue with the smell of freshly fried bacon in the air?

Chapter 19

Two heaping plates full of southern fried goodness later, we were finally on our way to see Arc. Mom called ahead to let them know we were coming.

As she put it, "You don't go calling on Lily without a proper warning first. Especially not with the goings on of late."

When we got there, the first thing Lily did was throw her arms around me. "I'm so very glad you're all right, child. I was so worried."

It took her words for me to realize that I hadn't called to let them know what had happened. Mom or Senior one must have filled them in. Either that or, like Opal, she had her own witchy ways of knowing things.

Arc gave me a hug, too, but it was a bit awkward. He kept glancing at Opie to see if there was a problem. I really didn't get it. I mean, he was my brother, right? What on earth would Opie have a problem with?

Once we were settled in the living room with glasses of Lily's special lemonade, I turned to Arc. "I want to know everything you know about Ryan's brother."

He shrugged. "I know he had a much rougher time at life than Ryan. I guess Ry really lucked out when it came to adoptive parents. Roger wasn't so lucky. He got in with a bad crowd, and things just snowballed from there."

Not at all sure that I believed in the whole blame it on the parents' thing, but I nodded all the same. "Did you ever meet him?"

Arc shook his head. "Never got the chance. Ryan only met him once that I know of. A week before Roger died."

It struck me odd that he said died rather than was murdered. Obviously, I wasn't the only one who felt that way.

"You do know that Roger was murdered, right?" Opie asked.

Arc's face kind of said it all. "No! He was murdered? How?"

The more important question to me was why had Ryan left out that little fact when telling Arc about it. Kind of need to know information, wasn't it?

"According to Opal, his head was bashed in like Sonya's. She's thinking maybe there is a connection between the two." I was trying to be gentle, but it was hard. Arc had to come to grips with all of this, and fast. We needed answers.

"But what connection could there possibly be . . ." He stared at us. "No way. Ryan did not do this. He loved Sonya like a sister. Hell, we grew up together, the three of us. He's a good guy." His eyes met mine dead on. "Ryan didn't do this."

I took a deep breath. Part of me wanted to point out that up until we'd found Sonya's ledger, he'd thought she was a good gal, too. That had been proven wrong pretty dang quickly. Maybe my brother just wasn't a very good judge of character.

Besides, Ryan hadn't made all that good of an impression on me the day before. Actually, he'd seemed more than a little like a jerk.

And that wasn't even taking into consideration that he had a key to pass through the high-powered Mineheart wards. After all, we only had his word that he had lost it.

I looked over at Opie. "We could use someone with a newspaper database brain when it comes to crime." In other words, we could use his dad. The man kept up to date on everything that was going on in the world of bad guys. I hoped that he didn't just keep that to a more local range.

He nodded. "I'll call him."

We waited. I wanted to ask him to put it on speakerphone, but I didn't think Sheriff Taylor would like that very much. He was a very private kind of guy.

"Hey, Dad, I got a question for you."

No hi, how are you doing? Geesh, men were so different from women, it was like they were a different species. It would have taken me at least three minutes of small talk to get to the meat of the call. Probably one of the reasons my cell phone bill was so high. I really needed to look into one of those unlimited plans.

Opie was quiet for a minute, listening and nodding. "I see. Well, off the top of your head, do you remember anything about a case down in Indianapolis? The murder of a man named Roger Hendrickson?"

More listening and nodding. At one point, I thought I saw Opie gulp, but he covered it well. By the time he hung up—again, without the girly preamble—I was bouncing on the balls of my feet. He knew something.

When he turned to me, his face had lost a bit of color. My bouncing stopped. I wanted good news, not bad. This looked bad.

"Dad isn't in the office today."

For once, Ruby stepped in. Odd for her. "So, what did he tell you?"

"Just that he'd check into it today and get with me tonight."

There was so much more to that phone call than that.

"Dang it," Arc said. Then he turned to Ruby. "Are you up for some computer research? I've been pretty limited as to how I can help up until now, but I'm great with a computer. If you're willing, the two of us should be able to track down the information we need pretty quickly."

Ruby glanced at me and then Opie. "Would you two be okay with that?"

Opie nodded, the color slowly coming back. "Sounds good to me. A division of work just makes sense at this point." He took my hand and started pulling me to the door. "Call us if you get anything."

They just nodded, already deep into the process of booting up their laptops. Never leave home without one. That was one of Ruby's rules. Of course, the bag she carried would hold a small horse. I went for light and easy, personally.

Lily followed us out. Once the door was shut, she turned to Opie. "Spill it."

Okay, so I wasn't the only one who noticed something was wrong with him.

He swallowed and then looked from Lily to me and back again. "It doesn't have anything to do with what's going on with Arc. I promise."

She tilted her head and raised one eyebrow. Yeah, I wasn't going to give him a pass on that one, either.

Finally, he took a deep breath. "Okay, look, Dad said he wasn't in the office. But he wasn't alone, either. I could hear someone talking behind him." This time the gulp was very evident. "It sounded a lot like Opal."

The gulp was catching. I knew I'd recognized that man's voice from my early morning call. Sheriff Taylor. And Aunt Opal? A shiver passed over me.

"It could be nothing more than him helping out a friend, right?" Opie sounded hopeful.

I hated to burst his bubble. Besides, I didn't feel right spilling the beans on them being together last night. For all I knew, they were in separate beds when I called. Not that I believed that for an instant, but it was a possibility. I kept my mouth shut on that.

Lily glanced back at the door. "I take it you don't want Ruby to know that your parents are together?"

"No, I don't. If they really are a . . . couple now, then they should be the ones to tell her. Right now, there isn't anything positive. Dad helps people. He's always been that way."

I felt Lily's gaze on me, but I couldn't meet her eyes. I don't know how she knew, but she did. Maybe Opal wasn't the only one who could read my thoughts.

"Very well," she said. "This is safe with me."

That's when I remembered the other part of my conversation with Opal from the night before. "Opal told me to ask Ruby to do personal protection spells on all of us, and offered any supplies we might need from the shop. I totally forgot to tell her."

I started back toward the door, but Lily stopped me. "You two go on. I think I know the spell she has in mind, and I've got everything here we'll need. It'll get done. You have my word." Then she turned and went back into the house, leaving me and Opie standing there on her front porch.

The sooner the subject was changed, the better. He must have felt the same way.

We almost made it out to the car before Ruby came running out of the house.

"Wait. You two need to know this!"

Opie pulled me to a stop, and we turned.

"The very first search we did on Roger Hendrickson listed his last employer. He worked for the Indianapolis division of Firestorm United."

I glanced back at the open doorway. Arc was standing there with an I told you so expression. I made a shooing motion for him to get out of sight. It wouldn't do for him to go showing himself now. Just because the council couldn't actually go into Lily's didn't mean they didn't have eyes watching her place.

But I got his point. Ryan Shea wasn't the only connection between the two murders. Stan Grayson was one too.

Now we were getting somewhere.

Arc whistled, and we walked back. I hoped whatever it was he had to tell us went quick. I wanted another run at Stan Grayson. And this time, I planned to stay until I'd gotten some answers.

"There's something else I just thought of," Arc said when we were back on the porch. At least he'd stepped out of the main doorway. Now he was hidden in the shadows from anyone more than a couple of feet away.

"A few months back, Sonya approached me with a business proposition from Grayson. He wanted to expand into home security. As he knew how to take houses down to the ground, he seemed to think he could do a pretty good job of protecting them from that too."

"Let me guess . . . he wanted your wards." I mean, at this point, it wasn't much of a guess.

Arc nodded. "Yup. And that means he knew about them and exactly what they could do." He paused. "And he knew about the keys too."

Okay, now I really wanted to talk to the man.

Chapter 20

"So how are we going to work this?" Opie asked.

We were parked outside the small office trailer of Firestorm United. Stan's truck was parked outside.

I chewed my lip for a minute, thinking it through. I knew that Opie wouldn't go for the whole impersonating a cop thing, but what if we didn't have to say anything? If he just assumed it, that wasn't on us, was it?

"The last time I was here, he thought I was with the police." Sure enough, Opie gave me a stern look. "Don't look at me like that. I did absolutely nothing to warrant him coming to that conclusion. All I did was ask about Sonya, and he kind of made the leap on his own. I think he has a major guilty conscience."

"Uh-huh," Opie said. He didn't look like he quite believed me.

I crossed my heart. It was a standard gesture, but one he knew I didn't take lightly. It was crazy but true. I'd never cross my heart on a lie, and he knew it.

"Okay, so your plan is to use that little fact today? Walk in there and pretend to be cops?"

"No. My plan is to walk in there and ask some very pointed questions. Like how much Grayson has to do with the Indianapolis division, and how well he knew Roger Hendrickson. If he wants to once again assume that we're on official police business, that's on him, right?"

Opie looked thoughtful. "It's a little shadier than I like. But I guess if we don't tell him I'm a deputy, that would be okay." He gave me a pointed look.

Once again, I crossed my heart, and he nodded.

"Okay, then. Let's do this." Then he hesitated as his hand reached for the door latch. "Just out of curiosity, do you have your taser with you?"

I patted my purse. "Never leave home without it." I'd learned that the hard way, one or two times too many.

He still wasn't moving. I got the hint.

Pulling the taser from my bag, I handed it over to him. He gave me a lopsided smile and shoved it into the waistband of his pants. Then he shrugged. "You have your magic if things go south in there. I feel better having something too."

That surprised me. I'd thought he was afraid I would use it without proper provocation. I'd never thought about the fact that I was asking the man to go in unarmed against a man who could quite possibly be a double-murderer.

What had I been thinking?

As we walked up to the trailer, I thought about what Opie had said. About how I had my magic if things went south. That was true, but the few times I'd used it had really put the fear of the Goddess into me. Things would have to go pretty darn south for me to risk using it again.

Then again, if Opie was in danger, all bets were off. I might think twice about using it to protect myself, but protecting Opie was another thing. That, I'd do without a second's hesitation. And that worried me. Funny, I'd much rather be the one with the taser.

I wouldn't kill anyone with that.

Unlike last time, my entrance into the trailer didn't get a smile. Grayson's eyes traveled over me and then Opie in turn.

"Kind of figured I hadn't seen the last of you," he said with a sneer. "Have you managed to come up with some kind of planted clue that somehow proves I'm the one who killed Sonya?" He gave a short bark of a laugh. "Wouldn't put it past you cops."

Opie raised an eyebrow but stayed silent. Good boy. As long as we didn't actually say we were cops, we shouldn't be able to be prosecuted for impersonating a law enforcement officer. There wasn't anything in the rule book that said we had to correct the man's assumptions. At least, I hoped there wasn't.

"We're just here to talk," Opie said, taking the lead. Fine with me. I was willing to bow to the fact that he had much more experience with this kind of thing than I did.

Grayson didn't bother to stand or offer us a chair, either. The man's manners were appalling. Then again, I could move faster if I was already standing, so that worked for me.

"And just what could you possibly want to know that I haven't told you a dozen times already? I didn't kill Sonya." He growled. Literally growled. "And yes, I'm aware that she made a complaint about me. A completely bogus one, too, if you want to know the truth. I never laid a hand on her. But she didn't get the raise she asked for, either, and revenge is a mother."

"Actually, right now, I'm more interested in your association with the Indianapolis division of the company. I believe you own both, don't you?"

Grayson went from looking annoyed to looking worried. His eyes went to his desk drawer. No way was he going to make it to open the thing.

Opie saw the glance too, and his hand moved under his jacket to rest on the taser. "Whatever's in that drawer, I suggest you leave it there." There was a touch of flint in Opie's tone. It was enough to convince Grayson that he meant business. Besides, the hand touching the taser was hidden from view. For all Grayson knew, it was a pistol instead of its non-lethal counterpart.

Not that being shot with a taser was anything to laugh about.

Grayson blew out a breath and leaned back in his chair. The fight seemed to drain out of him. "I didn't kill him, either, not that it will matter to you all."

"So, you're admitting that you knew Roger Hendrickson and the manner of his death?" Opie wanted the record straight.

The man nodded. "Yeah, I knew him. Briefly. He was a real piece of work, that guy. Made Sonya look like a saint, he did. That's saying something."

I had to agree with him there.

"Do you have any idea who did kill him? Is there someone else we should be questioning? Maybe someone with ties to both Roger and Sonya?"

His eyes glinted with what appeared to be hope. "Come to think of it, yeah, there is." He leaned forward, excited. "I'd forgotten about it, honestly, but I had to send Sonya down to help him on a job that was a little bigger than he could handle on his own. When she got back, she was acting real funny. I finally got the story out of her. This Roger guy was the spitting image of a friend of hers. Turns out they were brothers!"

Then his face fell. "Crap. I knew I should have gotten her friend's name. But you guys should be able to find him, right? I mean, surely you can get access to birth records and stuff like that, right?"

He really did look hopeful. I was almost ready to believe him myself. Right up until my eyes fell on the rack of keys hanging on the far wall. One of them was bright green.

I elbowed Opie and gave a short nod to the key rack. His eyes darted there and back to Grayson in a millisecond. Taking a deep breath, I clapped my hands.

The key started glowing, and precisely thirty seconds later, it whistled. Not a quiet one, either.

Grayson jumped out of his chair like he'd been shot from a cannon. "What the hell is that?"

"That, Mr. Grayson, appears to be the magicked key to Archimedes Mineheart's apartment." Opie paused, letting that information sink in. "You know . . . the place where the killer dumped Sonya Ignacio's body?"

He tried to run, but he didn't make it far. Not even to the door before he was on the ground twitching.

Opie disconnected the taser, flipped him over onto his stomach, then pulled out his cuffs. My eyebrow raised of its own accord. I hadn't known Opie had them with him. Trust him to bring the cuffs and not his gun. I'd be having a talk with him soon about that.

I didn't need a boyfriend who took stupid chances. One of us doing that was more than enough.

***

Things went pretty quickly after that, at least for a short time. Opie's friend from the local police force showed up with company, and they took Grayson into custody. Once we relayed the news about Hendrickson and the murder in Indianapolis, they didn't seem to have any doubts as to Grayson's guilt.

Neither did we.

It took quite some time at the local station going over our story not once but a good half-dozen times. We had no reason to lie. For me, it was a family matter that I was checking into, and for Opie, it was a matter of keeping his girlfriend out of trouble.

The fact that he was a sheriff's deputy in another county seemed to help. If I'd made the takedown on my own, I'd probably have been there a lot longer. And things wouldn't have gone nearly as smoothly as they did.

Once they had our statements and were satisfied that we weren't going to change our story even if they asked us to take it from the top one more time, we headed back to Lily's. By this time, it was late afternoon. The lawyer brothers were already off work and there.

I was a little surprised to see Merlin peeling potatoes in the kitchen. And he wasn't even complaining about it. In fact, he looked . . . happy. Part of that was knowing that Arc was finally a free man, but the other part had a lot to do with the woman chopping vegetables beside him.

There had to be a reason they weren't more open to the public about their relationship, but I hoped they got that sorted out soon. They deserved to be together. All the time.

I asked if there was anything I could do to help, but I got shooed from the kitchen.

"You go rest. You've done your work for the day."

That got a raised eyebrow from Merlin, but he never said a word. I grinned at him and left while the getting was good.

Opie and I sprawled out on the sofa, and I looked over at Arc and Ruby. They were sharing an oversized chair, looking particularly happy to have their bodies scrunched up together. Look at us, all coupled off. Lily and Merlin, Ruby and Arc, me and Opie, and soon, Mom and Archie. She just hadn't gotten there yet. Neither had Opal.

Not that it worried us. It wasn't seven yet. They still had a good half hour to make Lily's diner curfew.

Part of me wondered if Opal would come alone. I was betting the answer would be yes. As far as I was concerned, there wasn't any reason that she and the sheriff should have to hide their relationship, especially from us. I mean, they were both single adults. What was the harm? It wasn't like one of them was committing adultery or something. Opie's mom had left him years ago. So long ago, in fact, that I couldn't remember ever meeting her.

"Has anyone let the council know they've arrested Grayson for Sonya's murder?" I asked. "It would be nice to know they've given Arc a clean slate for the crime."

"I took care of that personally," Senior said, settling onto the arm of the couch. "Patty wasn't too pleased to hear it from me, but she verified it and called off the dogs." He looked over at Arc. "I'd be watching my p's and q's pretty closely for the next year or so. Once you're in the council's sites, they don't tend to let go all that quickly. Proven innocent or not, they'll be watching."

Arc swallowed but nodded. "I'll be careful."

"So," I said, going for nonchalant, "any chance we can break this binding tonight? Get your magical signature back to what it should be now that there isn't a reason not to?"

My brother gave a small shiver. "Sounds good to me. The sooner the better, in fact." I didn't understand the rather timid look he was giving me, as if we shared a secret or something. If it was the fact that I personally had no magic, it was hardly a secret to my family. It was something we'd all known for years.

I'd just never been totally okay with that fact before. Now I was more than okay with the thought of not having magic. The whole world would be a safer place once that was true again.

At five till seven, Senior glanced at his watch, looking a little worried. "It isn't like Sapphire to run this close without calling first."

When the knock came, he smiled and walked over to answer it. But it wasn't Mom; it was Opal.

And she didn't look happy.

Chapter 21

Opal walked straight over to Arc without sparing the rest of us so much as a glance. "We need to talk."

"O-okay," he said. "Can I ask what about?"

"How much do you know about Roger Hendrickson?"

He shrugged and looked over to me. "Not much. Just that he wasn't nearly as nice of a guy as Ryan, apparently."

"That's putting it mildly unless your friend was a multi-murdering conniving you know what too."

Arc's face blanched. "Multi-murdering? But I don't understand. He was killed before Sonya, wasn't he?"

"According to the police and medical reports, yes. But there are some things the police haven't been able to explain. Like why the blood and skin found under his fingernails match his own DNA but, other than his head wound and the burn on his wrist, there didn't appear to be a mark on him."

Ruby's eyes widened. She must have understood what Opal was saying, but I sure as heck didn't. "DNA is a singular thing, right? I mean, brothers wouldn't have the same DNA, would they?"

Opal's gaze never left Arc. "They would if they were identical twins. At least, close enough to fool the forensic team if they weren't alerted to the fact that they were dealing with twins."

Opie nodded. "There's a test now where they can melt DNA to distinguish between twins." He turned to me. "According to Grayson, Sonya had said that Roger was the spitting image of Ryan."

A feeling of dread started growing in my stomach. "Did you ask the police to run that DNA melt thing?"

"They are doing it now, as we speak. But they're a little too late."

Well, yeah, Sonya might still be alive if they'd known about the twin thing up front. But something told me that Opal meant more than that.

"Wait a minute," Arc said. "Now it sounds like you guys think Ryan had something to do with all this, but the killer was Grayson, wasn't it? He's the one in jail, isn't he? I don't care what you all think. Ryan isn't the killer. I don't care what the stupid DNA test comes back saying. He didn't do it."

Lily put her hand on Arc's shoulder. We had all jumped to the same conclusion, but it was pretty obvious that he hadn't made that leap yet.

It was kind of easy once you really thought about it. Especially with everyone who knew Ryan saying how much he'd changed since finding out he had a brother.

Arc looked back into Lily's eyes. "Ryan is innocent."

"No one is saying he isn't, dear," she said softly.

No. We were saying that Ryan Shea was currently resting in a mismarked grave somewhere. The man who had killed Sonya and tried to kill me was his brother.

Roger.

The instant he made the connection, he went white as a ghost. "Ryan's dead, isn't he?"

Opal nodded, not without compassion. "That would be my guess, yes. And since we know about Sonya's little secret gathering pastime, we can only assume that this time, it got her killed."

"Sonya wouldn't have tried to profit off Ry-Ry. She was even closer to him than I was. But it's possible she stumbled onto something and approached him about it."

"And that would have been enough to do it," Opal agreed. "From what I understand, you and Sonya were the only people really close to Ryan. Roger may have thought to eliminate both of you in one fell swoop. Sonya's murder, and your conviction for it."

Arc bent over and put his face in his hands. "They're both dead. My best friends in the entire world and they're both gone."

"It's understandable that you're upset, but we need every hand on deck right now, including you. We have a major problem."

Another one?

Senior stepped up. "Sapphire?"

Mom? What was he talking about? How could Mom be the problem?

"Her gem on my necklace went off about a half hour ago. She's in trouble. I'm guessing he has her."

My heart sank. "Can you find her?"

Opal nodded. "Yes, but I'll need to borrow Lily's lab. It was closer than the farmhouse."

"Follow me." Lily led Opal to a door I hadn't even noticed before, and they disappeared beyond it. From the sound of footsteps on stairs, it must lead down into the cellar of the house.

I was still in shock, finding it hard to breathe. Opie's arm reached around me and squeezed.

Ruby got up and picked up five small boxes from the entry table. "Better late than never, I guess," she said as she handed them out. "These are the spells Lily, Arc, and I did today. Personal protection spells. But these do more than just warn you of danger to yourself. They let you know when any of the others are in peril too."

"Opal said Mom's gem went off in her necklace. What exactly does that mean?" Please let it mean she was still alive and just needed help.

"Our moms did one of these spells ages ago. Opal added stones for me and you to her necklace as well. It's something I'd have done long ago, but it's a really hard spell to master. I couldn't have done it without Lily."

Each of the boxes held a small bracelet of gemstones threaded onto a simple golden chain. The sapphire on each of them was glowing. I touched it gently.

The other stones were normal looking. I could guess the identity of each of my family by color. That part was easy. We weren't the Gemstone Coven for nothing. But I wasn't so sure about the five remaining stones.

"Green is Arc, yellow is Senior, orange is Merlin, and the black is Lily." She looked over at me. "I wasn't so sure what color to make Opie's stone, so I went with gray."

I nodded. The color of stone didn't matter a bit as long as it glowed when it was needed. I couldn't take my eyes off Mom's glowing stone.

"Arc?" I asked quietly. "Where did Ryan live?"

Opie squeezed me tighter. "We can't rush into this, Amie. We have to have a plan first. Opal can find your mom with magic, right?"

Sure, but finding her wasn't the problem. The problem was finding her in time. By now, Roger probably realized he'd made a huge error in taking her. If he thought the police were convinced that Stan Grayson was the killer, then he would have no need to keep her alive as a bargaining chip with us.

I was pretty sure that was what he'd intended to use her as. Nothing more than a bargaining chip.

At least Senior was with me. He stood over me and reached down a hand. I took it.

"I'll take you there myself."

"Better yet, we'll all go." Opal and Lily came out of the doorway behind us. Opal glanced over at Arc. "Did Ryan live about five miles east of here?"

Arc nodded.

"Then that's where we are going to start." Opal's gaze fell on me. "That thing you did to Naomi Hill. Could you do it again?"

"Oh hell, yeah."

"Good. Just don't plan on me stopping you this time."

Chapter 22

We all piled into Lily's van and headed out. Ryan had lived in a small house just outside of town. The good thing for us was that he had no close neighbors and there were plenty of ways to sneak up on the house.

The bad thing was, they weren't there. They had been, though. The scent of Mom's perfume was still in the air.

"Can you revise the spell on the go?" Opie asked.

From the grim look on Opal's face, the answer to that one was no. But by then, I had a pretty good idea where Roger's next stop might be.

"We need to head to Firestorm. The warehouse," I said, already moving.

It didn't take long for everyone to get on the same page as me. All you had to do was put yourself into Roger's frame of mind. He'd taken Mom before he'd heard about Grayson's arrest. Now he had an eyewitness that he needed to get rid of. But if he used his normal method of brutally smashing in her skull, the cops might figure out they had the wrong man.

Little did he know that would soon happen, anyway. Just as soon as their forensics teams did that little DNA melting spell . . . or test, whatever.

The main thing here was that he would be looking for another way to get rid of her. And there was a warehouse filled to the brim with demolition supplies. Meaning, in all likelihood, a ton of explosives.

Senior took the keys this time, and we made it to the warehouse in nothing flat. A little magic might have been involved. He pulled into the parking lot for the warehouse, and we split up into teams of two. Opal and Ruby went to the left around the side of the building, and Senior and Arc headed to the right. Lily and Merlin were circling around to the back, and Opie and I were to take the front.

We were hoping at least one of the teams would reach her in time.

In fact, we all did.

But that had been his plan.

In the most unoriginal move ever, he'd tied Mom to a wooden office chair in the center of the big room. Once we were all gathered around her, getting her loose, he stepped out into view. When I saw how close he was to the doorway, I figured out his plan pretty quickly.

I think the others did too. The fact that he was waving a large detonator in his hand helped.

"Leave me. Run!" Mom yelled.

Even if that had been an option, which it certainly wasn't, it was far too late for that. Boxes and barrels of explosives surrounded us. If he set off just one, there would be nothing left here but a very large crater.

Opal stood and faced him. Ruby and I stepped up on either side of her. It would have been nice if we'd come up with a plan on our way here, but truthfully, all we'd been thinking of was getting to Mom in time. A little shortsighted now that we'd done that.

"I was kind of hoping you'd show up," Roger said, looking at me. "But I didn't know you'd bring the whole bloody gang. Well done! And thank you very much. You've made my job so much easier."

Opal was the first of us to speak. "You have no idea who or what you are dealing with, do you?"

His smile never faltered. "I've heard rumors and hints that the Minehearts are witches, but even if that's true, I don't think a bunch of people who love to dance naked around a bonfire under the full moon are anything for me to worry about."

I risked a glance at her. She was cool as a cucumber. Me? I was sweating like crazy, even with the draft on the back of my neck.

"Then you are a fool," Opal said. "Any one of us is more than a match for you. And to have gathered us all in one place? That only ensures your doom." Her voice was firm and steady. How did she do that?

"Funny," he said, waving the detonator once again. "I'm the one about to blow you all to kingdom come."

"Lily, how's that spell coming?"

"Almost there, just need a little more juice . . . ah, thank you, Merlin."

Roger actually laughed. "Should I be scared? What are you going to do? Turn me into a frog or something?" He grinned at us. "Can you do it before I press the button?"

"You press the button while you're still in here with us and you die too," I said, finally finding my voice. "If you were willing to do that, I don't think we'd all be here right now, would we?"

He shrugged. "Granted, I hope to be out the door first, but then, I'm closer than all of you."

And he turned and started running. Thing is, it's hard to run when your feet weren't making contact with the floor.

I was trying something new. I didn't just want to slam him into a wall. Not with what he held in his hand. So, I took him up instead.

My magic danced and sparkled around him as it lifted him up three feet off the floor and holding.

"How about now, Lily?" Opal asked, and for the first time, I heard the strain in her voice. Sure, she could handle a detonator-holding madman, but when her niece used powerful magic, she came a bit undone. Typical.

"Arc," I called out, "how you holding up?"

"I'm fine. If you need more juice, feel free to pull it."

As I watched the swirling, sparkling magic in front of me, I had to wonder just how much magic Arc had. Were all the Minehearts this powerful? If so, we Air witches wouldn't stand a chance against them in a fight.

It was a really good thing they were on our side. But I could see why up until now Opal had shied clear of them. Envy was a powerful thing too.

"Lily? How much longer?" Opal called.

I'd love to know what they were talking about, but I held my concentration on my magic. Too many stray thoughts wouldn't be good.

"Sorry, dear, I got a tad distracted. Just a second . . . got it!" Lily called back. "And Sapphire's free too. It's time to go."

"Drop him, Amie. We need to get out of here." Opal's voice was still sounding pinched.

But the magic didn't want to let him go. It wanted to squeeze him until every last ounce of breath had left his body, and then squeeze some more. It wanted to end him.

Or maybe that was just me. The man had tried to kill Mom. He needed to die.

"Arc?" Opal said. "We might need you up here."

He was beside me in an instant, his hand resting on my elbow. I felt the magic start to ebb out of me. He was pulling it back to him.

Within seconds, Roger fell to the ground. He must have had a little cat in him, because he hit the ground on his feet and running.

Once again, he didn't get far. Opie hit him with the taser, and he did what anyone hit by a taser would do. He went down.

"Stop or I'll shoot," Opie called out softly as he disconnected the prongs. Then he looked at the detonator and back at Opal. "Why didn't that thing go off?"

"Lily's got it in a technology lock, but those spells don't usually last long. We have to get out of here now."

Opie nodded and reached down, picking Roger up and throwing him over his shoulder in a fireman's carry. If I hadn't been so distracted, I might have found it hot to see him using such strength.

But right now, I was having a hard time just standing. The ability to think and feel was quickly leaving me too.

Arc copied Opie's move, and the next thing I knew, my head was dangling halfway down his back. And we were moving. Fast.

We made it to the van, but barely.

"The spell is slipping!" Lily cried out.

"Minehearts to the front."

Arc dropped me to the ground. I was pretty impressed that I had managed not to lose consciousness this time. Maybe my use of magic was improving. If only I could learn how to stop using it when the time was right.

I knew I should be scared, but all the emotion had drained out of me with the magic. I watched the scene unfold like a television drama.

The three Minehearts ran to the front of the van just as the first, smaller explosion hit. They formed a short line to the side of the van, holding hands with Arc in the middle.

I wanted to go to help, but I couldn't get my legs to work right. Watching was all I could do, and that wasn't any help at all.

Merlin and Senior held up their non-holding hand toward the warehouse, and all three of them were chanting. As for the rest of us, the other women were already in the van, and Opie was trying his best to stuff me in there too. I was fighting him. I felt like I had to be here, out in the open.

I could feel the power still ebbing out of me, and I didn't want anything between me and Arc but air. I'd taken his magic, and he needed it right now more than ever before.

Then the main blast hit. There were a lot of explosives in that building, and they all seemed to be set off pretty much instantaneously. One second, there was a warehouse standing there, and the next, all that could be seen was a massive ball of fire.

The shockwave of the blast knocked us all back five feet or more, including the van. But the men were still standing and chanting.

Debris started raining down, but not a single piece of it hit us or the van. When the wave was over, and it didn't take long, the parking lot and everything in it had been obliterated. All but a small rectangle covering the area of the van's parking space and the people still outside it. Not a scratch.

Dang, those Earth witches were powerful. Protection was their thing, yeah, but . . . well, dang.

By this time, I was kind of going in and out brain-wise. Truthfully, I might have blacked out a second or two here and there, but not the total faint as before when I'd done something with major magic.

I was awake when Senior and Merlin turned to Arc.

"What the hell was that?" They looked surprised for some reason. I couldn't fathom why.

Arc was still staring at the building as they released each other's hands. "I tried to tell you. Amie is special."

Me? What the heck did I have to do with this?

The two men turned toward me with a look of almost horror. What the hey?

I used the last of my strength to give them a small two-finger wave. I'd have added a smile in for good measure, but my face wasn't working, either.

Then I did what I'd been so proud of myself for not doing.

I passed out.

Chapter 23

This time was much different than the last two times I'd passed out because of magic. For one, I'd managed to hang on for longer, but that had come at a price it seemed.

When I woke up this time, it was to a feeling of extreme thirst and hunger. A glance around showed that I was back at the farmhouse and in my own bed.

As soon as I opened my eyes, Ruby—who'd been sitting in a chair beside the bed—called down to Opal. "She's awake."

I heard thundering footsteps running up the stairs, and Arc and Opie came in through the door into my kitchen area. Both of them were grinning.

"Thank the Goddess!" Arc said, coming over to hold my hand. "I thought I'd killed you."

I opened my mouth to ask him why on earth he would have thought that, but just then, Mom rushed into my room and gathered me into a fierce hug. It's hard to talk when your entire face was pressed into someone's bosom. And Mom's was somewhat larger than most.

The moment passed. Opal pushed her way through to me with a bottle of ice-cold water. "Drink this."

She didn't have to tell me twice. I downed it in mere seconds. It helped, but now my stomach rumbled. It wanted its little piece of the pie too. Ooh, pie!

Opie laughed. "I think we'd better get her something to eat too."

I grinned at him. "Yes, please."

Even with the hunger and thirst, I didn't have the lingering headache that I had experienced before. Well, I had a bit of a headache, but it was dull, not the sharp pain like before.

Grimacing up at Opal, I had to ask. "How long was I out?"

"Two days and . . ."—she glanced over at the clock—"two hours."

What? I was stunned. No wonder I felt so rested.

"What happened?"

"The boy drained you completely," Opal said with a nasty glance at Arc. "A witch needs a little magic just to survive. Your body took the time it needed to heal. It just needed every ounce of resources you had available. Hence the whole unconscious thing."

"I'm really sorry, Amie." That was Arc. "I panicked and took more from you than I should have. We really need to get this binding broken before I hurt you." He gave me a sad smile. "Being bound to you is almost like a drug. I just can't seem to get enough power."

I wanted to know what the heck he was talking about, but the larger—and much hungrier—part of me wanted food. Any food, though pie would be nice, as that thought had already crept into my brain.

"Okay. All people with dangly parts between their legs need to leave my bedroom so I can get up and get dressed." Normally things like that didn't bother me. After all, I was a witch and totally fine with dancing naked around a bonfire under the light of the moon. But I didn't want Opie's first time seeing me without my clothes on to be like this.

Opie and Arc went into the kitchen area—hopefully one of them would have the forethought to start making me something to eat. Although, with my grocery buying habits, there wasn't likely to be anything there to fix.

When the door shut behind them, I jumped up and hurriedly put on jeans and a T-shirt. I had to admit that my brain was pretty much solidly fixated on food, so Opal's question caught me totally off guard.

"How long have you had magic like that? And why did you keep it from us?"

I felt the frown form even as I tilted my head toward her. "Huh?" Eloquent, I know. That's me in a nutshell. A gal great with words.

"Opal, this isn't the time or place for this conversation," Mom said. "Give her time and let's get some food into her. Then we'll all sit down and have a nice little chat about where to go from here."

I'd always thought Opal was the dominant one of the sisters, but not this time. Then again, I was Mom's daughter. Her word should be the deciding factor in anything regarding me.

I wanted to know what was going on, and why everyone seemed to think that life-saving magic had come from me, when I knew it had been Arc's power to begin with. But first . . . food.

When we came out into the kitchen, I smelled the most heavenly of scents. "Is that . . .?"

"Carnie's pizza with bacon and mushrooms. Freshly nuked to just the right warmness, too." Opie grinned at me. "I wanted you to wake up to something good."

I returned his grin and dug in. The others just watched. It was probably quite a sight. I wasn't that graceful of an eater when I wasn't starving. Now? All that mattered was getting food into me as quickly as possible.

And soda. That helped too. As I ate and drank, the dull headache subsided too. I felt great. Possibly better than I had ever felt in my entire life.

And after demolishing a full half of a large Carnie's pizza, I was finally ready for the talk.

***

Unfortunately, the others weren't ready for me. Not quite yet.

It appeared as though now my family had grown substantially. It wasn't just the four of us Ravenswinds anymore. We had others. They might not all be related to us by blood, but they were family all the same. Mom had seen to that for most of them.

And Opie, well, Opie was staying too. If he was going to be a big part of my life—which I fully intended—then he needed to stay up to date on what was going on in the witchy world. It was important. There was also the possibility that including him would help ease his shock and awe syndrome too. It was just magic, after all.

While we set up some extra chairs and got ready for our other guests, the others filled me in on what all I'd missed the last couple of days.

They had charged Roger Hendrickson with the two murders. That special forensic DNA test had been done, and it was pretty proof-positive that he was guilty of the crime. And, as he had access to the key to Arc's apartment, it was easy to guess that it wouldn't take long for the police to gather the needed evidence to slam dunk Sonya's murder on him as well.

As for Stan Grayson, he didn't quite receive the get out of jail free card that you might have expected him to.

The local police force had used his charge to get a search warrant for his home and business. Grayson was into some pretty nasty stuff. Enough to keep him locked up for quite some time.

Once the trial was done, of course. The man had money and had already made bail. Personally? I kind of hoped he jumped it. It would be fun going after that slimeball. After all, I hadn't even gotten to use the taser on him. That had been all Opie.

On an unrelated note, I knew what I was getting my new boyfriend for Christmas this year.

With their normal perfect timing, Lily drove up in her shiny, undamaged van, and she and the two older Minehearts climbed out.

After everyone got settled into seats with drinks, Opal turned to me once again. No more putting this off.

It was time. I decided to take the lead.

"Before you say anything, yes, I do remember the question you asked earlier. And for the record, I don't have a clue what you're talking about." I glanced over at the Minehearts. "Opal seems to think I have this massive amount of magic and that I might have been hiding it from her all these years. How ridiculous is that? Would one of you guys please tell her that I was only pulling the magic from my familiar." I gave Arc a small smile. "Sorry about that, by the way. That much magic being pulled had to hurt."

My brother—boy, did I like calling him that—was giving me an odd look. "What the bloody heck are you talking about? I pulled magic from you."

"But the magic you pulled back was the power I'd already drained off you." I mean, come on, if there was one thing I was fairly sure of in my life, it was that I had about as much magic as a toaster.

Not that toasters weren't great. Who didn't like toast? But they just weren't magic.

"We seem to have a difference of opinion here." Mom stepped in before Opal could get anything out. "I think the easiest way to solve the problem would be to do the unbinding. Then, if Amie keeps her magic, the riddle will be solved. At least in part."

Opal hesitated but finally nodded. "I guess that makes sense." She looked over to me and Arc. "Are the two of you up for this?"

I glanced at Arc and smiled. "I'm ready to go back to the old Amie at any time. As long as we're sure that doing this won't hurt you."

He swallowed and nodded. Everyone knew that a familiar binding was usually a life-long thing. There was a reason for that. Breaking the binding was considered to be a death sentence for the familiar. Not something a witch would take lightly. Especially one with a familiar who happened to be another witch.

"He should be fine," Lily said. "I've checked his cat over very closely, and she doesn't seem to have suffered any damage from the unbinding. It appears the trick is to just form another binding rather than trying to undo the first." She snapped her fingers. "Which reminds me."

Merlin nodded and went out to the van. When he returned, he had a large cat carrier filled with Momma cat and her three little kittens.

"Time to choose your real forever familiar, dear," Lily said softly. "I thought one of the young ones might do nicely."

I nodded, strangely choked up for some reason. "Can I take a minute to choose?"

"Take all the time you need, dear. Even if we do know now how to undo a binding, it isn't something to be done lightly. There has to be some repercussions from it."

"Repercussions?" Arc's voice squeaked just a bit.

She patted his hand. "Don't worry, dear. We'll help the two of you through this, no matter what happens."

Arc's gaze met mine. Suddenly, neither one of us were in too big of a hurry to do this.

Not dying was good, yes. But neither of us liked the idea of possible repercussions. The guilt started flooding in again. I'd done this to him.

I hoped if there were repercussions, they would affect me, not him. He hadn't asked for this.

Chapter 24

The backyard wouldn't do for Opal. No, we all had to traipse all the way into the woods and up to the hilltop where we held our monthly full-moon meetings.

I understood her reasoning. There was a lot of power in that place. And an almost overwhelming presence of the Goddess too. Kind of one and the same, when you really thought about it.

Once we all made it to the top, they instructed me to create a circle. Arc stayed out of it, but my soon-to-be new familiar and I were dead center of it. I'd decided on the calico kitten.

Or rather, it had decided on me. We'd let them out to play and explore, and the other two had run off and started checking things out pretty thoroughly. Normal little kitten behavior. The tiny calico headed straight my way. She climbed up in my lap and settled in, content to just watch the antics of the others.

Seemed like a fit to me.

"Do you remember the spell?" Ruby asked.

I nodded. It was ingrained on my very soul.

The calico kitten was already in my lap, purring up a storm. I looked down at her and smiled. Who knew I could be a cat person?

A glance at Arc to be sure he was ready for whatever might come, and I spoke the magical words that would bind us forever.

I pledge to thee my life and love
Through thick and thin, magic and blood.
Bound to you and you to me,
Forever more, so shall it be.

This time, I was paying more attention as I bent down to kiss the little furry head. I saw the blue magic form around us, connecting us.

The little kitten raised her eyes to mine, and I swear upon the Goddess, she smiled at me. Cats can do that?

A cough brought me back to the reality of the time. Arc. I turned to him with my heart in my throat, but he looked fine.

"How are you?" I asked.

He swallowed, his Adam's apple bobbing up and down. "It feels weird, but I'm okay, I think. Just a little . . . empty, I guess is the best way to describe it."

"So, don't you think your new familiar needs a name?" Lily asked.

I was thinking about going with Destiny, but that didn't seem right. After all, that had been the name I had used for Arc's cat form. Back when he'd been a cat.

I like Destiny.

The three words weren't actually words. More a very strong feeling that I was having a hard time describing, even to myself. The one feeling them. I glanced down at the little creature in my lap. She blinked up at me and tilted her tiny head at me.

"Destiny?" I made it a question, and I got my answer too. She purred even louder and rubbed her tiny little noggin against my arm.

Destiny it was, then.

"Kind of unoriginal, but hey, what do I know?" Arc was grinning when he said it, so no hard feelings there. Besides, he hadn't been too fond of the name when I'd used it on him.

"Okay, I know we should give you time to get familiar with your new . . . well, familiar," Opal said. "But this magic thing has been driving me crazy."

She did a brief chant and then nodded. "The binding between you and your brother has been well and truly severed, child. Now pull some magic—but slowly. Try something small this time." She gave me a smile. "Even if that hasn't exactly been your way of doing things up till now."

She wasn't wrong. It seemed my magic didn't do anything halfway.

I took a deep breath and handed Destiny to Ruby, outside of the circle. Then I concentrated and tried to pull a tiny bit of magic from the air surrounding us. Nothing. Looking over at Opal, I shook my head.

"I'm sorry. There's nothing there."

Her chin jutted out. "Oh, there's something there all right. You just have to find it." She took a step toward me, but Mom reached out a hand to stop her.

"My daughter, my way."

Opal didn't look too happy, but she nodded.

Mom smiled at me and stepped into my circle, reaching down to re-activate it. "Now, dear, I want you to do exactly what I say, all right?"

I nodded. She was my mom. If I couldn't trust her, who could I trust?

"Close your eyes and feel the air surrounding you." I did. After a full minute had passed, she said, "Now feel the air giving you a touch of its power. Let it flow into you."

I tried, but again, nothing. I was back all right. Right back to my non-magical self.

Then Senior stepped up to the circle. "May I?"

Mom's eyes widened and glanced over at Opal, who didn't look at all happy now. But Mom nodded, and she and Senior changed places. Now it was him in the circle with me.

It felt a bit awkward. I knew now that he was my dad, but it still didn't feel right to me. Taking a deep breath, I waited.

He smiled at me. "Do you trust me, dear?"

I thought about it and finally nodded. I trusted Mom, and if she trusted him, that was good enough for me.

"Okay, then here's what I want you to do. Concentrate and release the touch of air's magic."

I raised an eyebrow at him. What air magic? But to humor him, I went through the motions, anyway. Again, nothing. But at least that was expected this time.

"Now, take my hand." I did. "Close your eyes and imagine the earth beneath you."

I might be slow on the uptake, but I finally got it. The fact that Senior was my father, coupled with the look of distaste on Opal's face, could only mean one thing. They thought I was an Earth witch. When I thought about it, it kind of made sense. Who said a gal couldn't get her magic from her father?

Sending my thoughts deep into the earth under my feet, I reached out my magical fingers for a sign of . . . anything. This time, I'd admit I was a little disappointed. It would have been nice to have just a touch of magic. But, no. Nothing.

Now everyone was looking at me. I shrugged.

"I tried to tell you all. I pulled the magic from him." I pointed to Arc. "Now do you believe me?"

The others looked confused, but when my eyes hit Lily's face, they stopped dead. She didn't look confused; she looked scared. That terrified me even more than when Opal had felt that way. Lily didn't seem to get scared, not even when facing almost certain death.

Only now she was. And it had something to do with me.

When Senior went to step out of the circle, Lily held up a hand. "Wait." Her eyes held mine. "For this next thing, I want you to think very, very small. I want you to grab hold of just a wisp of air magic. Don't try to grab a whole handful, just a hair's breadth."

I frowned at her, but it was Lily, so I lifted my hand and pinched the air in front of me. That should do it.

"Good. Now, with your other hand, touch your father's arm. Use him to connect with the earth. Again—and I can't stress this enough—pull a tiny little bit of Earth's magic. Think of holding a few grains of dirt in your hand."

My frown only deepened, but I did as she said.

Or rather, I tried to. As soon as I connected to the Earth magic while holding on to that of Air, magic started flooding into me. Senior stepped away quickly, but it was too late, my body had made the connection it needed.

Arc had been right. The power hadn't been his. It had been mine.

What I didn't understand was why that fact seemed to terrify everyone around me. Having magic was a good thing, wasn't it? Wasn't that what Opal had wanted for me all along?

"By the God and Goddess," Mom whispered. "She's a Light Witch."

I looked over at Opie. At least there was one person in the group who was as clueless as to what that meant as I was.

"What's a Light Witch?" I asked. Witches matched the elements they got their power from. But I only knew of Air, Earth, Fire, and Water. Where did Light factor into it? It wasn't an element, was it?

"A Light Witch is a very powerful being, dear, which explains a lot," Lily said slowly. Then she looked around the group, making sure to meet everyone's eyes as she did. "But for now, I think it's a very good idea that no one mentions this to the council."

"Mentions what to the council?"

We all whirled around to see Patricia Bluespring stepping into the clearing behind us.

Crapsnackles, but I had a very bad feeling about this.

Chapter 25

"Patty, what are you doing here?" Senior forced the words out with a smile. That had to be hard.

She stood a little taller. "I'm here because Opal invited me. When there was no one at the farmhouse, I went out back and heard noise coming from up here." She shrugged. "So I came."

We all looked to Opal.

"Yes, I invited her. And then I got so caught up in other things that I totally forgot about her coming." She turned to her visitor. "I'm sorry. Let's go back down to the house. I have something for you."

Patricia stood firm. "Before we go, I'd like my question answered. What is no one to mention to the council?"

For what it was worth, Opal never batted an eye. Instead, she shrugged and shook her head.

"Personally, I don't see any reason to hide it from the council any longer."

"Opal . . ." Lily's voice was quiet, but there was a lot of stress behind that one word.

"Don't worry, Lily, I think the witches' council will understand that Amie truly thought Archimedes Junior was a cat at the time." She turned to Patricia. "That's the reason none of us could lock onto Arc here. He turned himself into a cat to get away from us, and then Amie found him in an animal shelter and adopted him."

Patricia's eyes widened. "She made another witch her familiar?"

The woman was smart. She didn't have to have someone dot the I's and cross the T's for her.

"Yes, but as Opal said, you really can't say that I did anything wrong. He was a cat at the time. I had absolutely no way to know otherwise."

"Seems funny that the single witch you 'accidentally' made into your familiar just happened to be your brother."

"She didn't find that out until much later," Mom said. "Archie and I kept that from her all these years." Her eyes drifted over to Opal and back. "We know it isn't really an accepted practice for Air and Earth to mingle." Her back straightened. "But I think that's more than a bit racist of everyone."

Patricia looked around the group. Opal had been smart. With her cover story, everyone here had a right to look a little guilty. Hopefully, it would be enough to appease the woman.

I wasn't all that sure why Lily thought we should hide me being a Light Witch, whatever the heck that entailed. But I was quite sure she had her reasons.

The council woman thought about it for a minute, then gave a small nod. "All right, then. The matter is closed." She fixed her gaze on Opal. "But that would be a different story if he had ended up being guilty, you know."

Opal nodded. "The Goddess works in mysterious ways. Somehow, she wanted Arc and Amie together. It's just too coincidental to be anything other than the Goddess' own hand at work."

Patricia took a deep breath and rubbed her temples. "Okay, I'm ready to go back to the house now."

***

The first thing Patricia noticed when she walked in was the kittens. We had forgotten to cage them back up and had left them roaming freely in Mom's apartment.

The little white one walked right up to the woman and started trying to climb her pants leg. She bent down and picked it up, snuggling it into her chest.

"What a beautiful creature, Opal. I don't suppose you'd be looking for a home for her?"

"Actually, you'd have to ask Arc about that. The momma cat used to be his familiar, so technically, these little gals are his too."

She seemed disappointed, but she set the kitten back down on the floor. "Oh. I see."

The kitten stayed right by her foot, unmoving.

"She's yours if you want her," Arc said gently. "It would appear she has chosen you. That's a good sign for a witch. Are you needing a familiar?"

Patricia's eyes grew watery. "I lost my Frankie Cat three weeks ago. That's part of the reason I threw myself into this case so hard. Well, that and . . ."

"And the fact that it involved us Minehearts," Senior said.

She looked away but nodded.

"Amie told me what you said about your granddad's pocket watch. I didn't keep it, Patty. I returned it the day after you left. Gave it to your new roommate to pass on to you. I'm so sorry. I should have made sure to hand it to you directly. I know how much it meant to you."

Patty sat down hard in one of Mom's easy chairs. That gave the little white kitten enough leverage to make the climb up and into her lap. She stroked her absently.

"That would have been my cousin Talia. I didn't stay with her long. She wasn't a very good person."

"Well, we can't change the past," Opal said, handing Patricia a small jeweler's box. "But we can fix things in the present."

Her forehead wrinkled as she opened the box. I leaned over just enough to see inside it. A beautiful pocket watch sat inside the silk-lined box.

Patricia lifted the watch out of the box by the chain. "But I thought you said . . ."

"Your roommate sold it to a local pawnshop. It took me a few days to track it down, but I did." Opal looked over at Senior. "By the way, you owe me fifteen hundred dollars."

He nodded. "Not a problem."

Now the tears were flowing in earnest. "All these years . . ."

Mom gave Senior a little push, and he walked over and knelt down in front of her. "Maybe now we can put all that behind us and be friends again? I think the watch and the kitten would make a good start for that."

She nodded. "I'd like that."

There wasn't much more to say after that. Ruby went upstairs and got Yorkie Doodle's carrier for Patricia to take home her new kitten, and a few minutes later, she left.

I'd waited long enough.

"Why can't we tell the council I'm a Light Witch?"

The End... for now.

But the story continues in Book Three: <u>Un-Familiar Magic</u>. Release Date: October 1st, 2019.

A Note From Belinda

Thank you so much for reading Relatively Familiar. I truly hope you enjoyed it! Please check out my website at BelindaWrites.com for updates on upcoming books.

Also, if you can spare a few minutes, please consider giving my book a review. I'd really appreciate knowing what you thought of it.

Belinda White
August 2019

Other Books by Belinda White

Accidental Familiar Series:

All Too Familiar

Relatively Familiar

Un-Familiar Magic (October 2019)

Benandanti Series:

Finders Weepers

Sister's Keepers

Demon Peepers

Manufactured by Amazon.ca
Bolton, ON